MISSING

in

CANCUN

RONALD DEAN DURBIN

ISBN: 978-1-63950-301-8 (sc)
ISBN: 978-1-63950-302-5 (e)

Writers Apex

Gateway Towards Success

8063 MADISON AVE #1252
Indianapolis, IN 46227
+13176596889
www.writersapex.com

CONTENTS

This book is dedicated to
my siblings and their better halves.

Saturday,
SEPTEMBER 2, 2000

J ack couldn't sit still. His daughter's flight was ten minutes late, and he didn't like it. He was able to control most things around him. He was the CEO of his own company, and people hopped when he told them to. Jack's company owned 25 percent of Americana South, but he couldn't get the plane to land any quicker.

Sara and two friends had gone to Cancun their last week of summer break. Wednesday of next week, she would begin Freshman Orientation at New York City University. His little girl had grown up while he was amassing a small fortune. This week taught him that his time with his daughter was very limited, and he needed to enjoy these next few years because after college, she could end up anywhere.

Now the plane was twenty-seven minutes late. Jack tried pacing, but that didn't make the plane come down either. He walked to the window to look again, only to be staring right at it. Others began to move around to prepare to greet their family or friends. Some held up signs with names. Jack didn't have to get ready. He was ready to give his big girl a hug and offer supper to her two friends.

Jack had a driver, but he had given Tony the night off. He wanted to drive his daughter home and not worry about making Tony work extra. He had agreed to take Jessie and Mel home as well. This would be a fun night. Victor would have to hold down the fort on Monday because Jack would be staying home Sunday and Monday. But tonight he was going to have dinner with his daughter and her friends. Kate was at a fund-raiser for New York kids at risk, so she wouldn't be joining them.

As his mind raced on, people passed. Others got hugs. A few of the sign people found whom they were looking for, but Sara hadn't come out of the walkway. Just when he moved to ask if that was everyone, he saw a movement. It was Mel. Her hands were covering her face, and she wouldn't look at Jack. He moved to her, slowly. She seemed to be in another world. When he spoke, she didn't hear. Gently, he took her wrist and asked, "What's happened, Mel? Where are Jessie and Sara?"

Mel only made a whimpering noise while not removing her hands. Jack saw that there was a real problem. He asked to verify that Jessie and Sara were not on the flight. Jessie and Sara had not gotten on the flight in Cancun.

"I'm going to need an office. Something has happened, and we don't need to stay out here in the open. Also, book me a ticket on the return trip."

"Yes, Mr. Fitzgerald. Follow me, please." Alice led Jack and Mel to a private office just a few steps away.

Jack gently put his arm around a sobbing Mel. She now clung to him as if he were a big teddy bear. When they reached the office, Alice let them go in and then said, "If you need anything, I'll be right outside the door."

She wasn't expecting Jack to say anything, but he did. "Alice, bring Mel some water, and I'm going to need a martini."

"Yes, sir."

Jack pulled out his cell phone and dialed Victor.

Caller ID told Victor Madden that his friend and boss was calling. This would not be a social call at this time of the evening. "Hello, boss. Just can't get along without me, huh?"

"Yes, Victor. You guessed it. I need a favor. I'm at JFK, and Sara didn't come in on the plane. I'm going to fly down there and find out why. It's not likely she would just miss her flight. Something's really wrong. Mel came back, but she's not talking yet. Anyway, I'll need you to come here and take her home. Then you'll need to tell her parents what you know. I need you to call Jessie's parents as well and then let Kate know. I may be a few days. I'll stay in touch with you and keep you updated. Yes, I'll call Kate as soon as I know something. Are you getting this?"

"I'm on my way, Jack. Be careful. Don't reveal too much to anyone about why you are there. Go low profile."

"Good idea. Sorry, friend, for bothering you. I want you to put the jet crew on standby. We might fly home tomorrow. I just have no idea what's going on. If the jet comes down, Kate might want to come. We just need to keep in touch."

"I'll take care of things here. If you don't mind, I'll give Frank a heads-up that you might be out of town for a couple of days."

"Sounds good. Bye."

The lack of attention had allowed Melissa to recoup. "Mr. Jack, I think I can talk with you now."

She revealed that Sara hadn't come home like they had agreed. Mel and Jessie just thought Sara was fooling around. When she didn't come home in the morning, they began backtracking. Then it was time to catch the plane. Mel left, and Jessie stayed to wait for Sara to show up. That's all she could tell for the time being.

Most of the time, Kate and Jack lived in Glen Cove up on the northern beach area on Eastland Drive, but he also had an apartment in the city. Victor lived in Queens, so he would be arriving soon. Mel stayed with Alice while they waited for Victor to show up.

The flight to Cancun was too long. It allowed Jack's mind to wonder about too many bad things that could have happened to his little girl. The third martini put Jack to sleep for the last hour. A tap on the shoulder told him it was time to put his tray up and his seat in the upright position in preparation for landing.

A limo was waiting for Jack as the plane landed. He didn't have to clear customs at all. He went straight to the Grand Palace Hotel, a four-star hotel on the beach. His company also owned stock in the Grand Palace Hotel. He had the Presidential Suite at the regular room rate. Jessie knew he was coming and was there to meet him.

Jessie was really ready to see a familiar face. She ran to him and hugged him and held on and then said, "Hi, Uncle Jack."

"Hi, honey. How're ya doin'?"

"I'm so worried. Sara would never do this. Something has happened to her . . ." Jessie couldn't talk. She cried like a little child cries after they fall. They wait until they've run into the house and are holding on to Mom to cry. Jack led her to a sofa, and they sat.

Jack just stroked her hair and waited. Jessie somehow felt responsible for her friend not returning. After she was all cried out, Jack still held her.

"We'll get to the bottom of this tomorrow. For now, let's go to bed. Have you called your parents?"

"Yes, sir."

"Do you want to stay in your room, or do you want to come to my suite?"

"I'm okay. All my stuff is there."

"Okay, Jessie. I'm going to make a few phone calls back home and then turn in. Good night."

"'Night. Thanks."

After Jack checked in, he dialed Kate's phone but wasn't sure how she would be reacting.

"Jack, where are you?"

"Victor should have told you that I was flying to Mexico. Mel didn't know what had happened to Sara, so I'm here to find out."

"Are you at the Palace?"

"Yes. I told Victor to get the jet ready to fly. When I know something, I'll call. Go ahead and tell Jere that his sister is missing in Cancun and that I'm here to do whatever I can. I suggest not telling anyone else. Tell one or two people, but if this is a kidnapping, we'll need to go low profile."

"Do you want me to fly down tomorrow?"

"I really don't know what else you could do, except be here for me. Jere starts school in a couple of days, so he needs to be there. It's probably best if you stay there. It won't feel good, but I think it's the best thing."

"You're right. It doesn't feel good, but I agree with you."

"'Night, honey."

"'Night."

Jack dialed Victor's number, knowing he wouldn't go to sleep until he had heard from Jack. "Hello, Victor."

"Hi, Jack. Mission accomplished here. We'll hold the jet ready for a trip to Mexico. How are you doing?"

"Not good. I've started thinking about all of the things that could have happened to Sara, and none are good. I'm going to drink another martini and go to bed. We'll start checking on things tomorrow."

Sunday,
SEPTEMBER 3, 2000

I t wasn't a good night. Jack kept his eyes closed, but he tossed and turned. He missed his daughter and was wondering what might have happened to her. But he was also evaluating his job as a father. He had provided a good lifestyle for his children, but he hadn't been in the picture very often. Making his company successful had been the most important thing in his life. Even as a husband, he hadn't really been there for Kate.

With the morning came a new Jack. The company would come second in his life from this point on. He would give his wife and children the attention they deserved. At this thought, he cried, knowing it was too late for Sara.

After a while, he rolled over and out of bed. He didn't want the day to begin. Looking around Cancun would be great. The reason would be wrong. It was time to call Jessie.

"Good morning, Jessie."

"Good morning, Uncle Jack. I'm hungry."

"Good. I'll meet you in the café."

"All right."

Jack loved young people, but he just hadn't taken time to be with his. When he saw Jessie, she looked much better. Being a man, he didn't know her makeup hid much of her concern. She came over and hugged him, and it made both of them feel better.

They were both hungry, and the restaurant buffet took care of them. Jack was amazed at how strong and good the coffee was. It wasn't the coffee or the buffet, but there seemed to be something magical about Cancun. Jack didn't know if it was the beach, the sun, the warm weather, or just what. But now it was time to implement the plan. The plan was to visit the local police station and talk only with the chief.

Noe Diaz had worked his way up to number 2 in the department. He was selling and buying. He played the game and danced the dance. His last two promotions had come after some unfortunate accidents. Visiting his boss was not fun but necessary. "Hello, Capitan Sanchez. How's it going?"

"Did you find out anything on the ATM robberies?" Captain Sanchez hated Lieutenant Diaz.

"Not yet."

"Are you working on it?" He didn't want to chitchat with Diaz any more than he wanted to stick his hand into pig slime.

"Of course, I am."

"So why are you here bothering me? Go do your job."

"Capitan, you don't like me very much."

"I don't like you at all. You are dirt. You are a dirty cop. You were involved with two accidents that got you your last promotion, but I just can't prove it. When I can prove it, you'll join your friends in jail. If I can't prove it, then I'll probably have an accident as well."

"Capitan, you don't have to go anywhere."

"Yes, I know. Just don't look while some crimes are being committed. Get your stinking carcass out of my sight before I squash a roach."

"That sounds like a threat to me."

The captain stood up and moved toward Lieutenant Diaz, and Noe dashed out. He couldn't scare someone who was not afraid of him.

Pedro Salas hated Noe, knowing he was on the take. "Hey, Lieutenant, did you and El Capitan have a lovers' quarrel?"

"One day, Salas, your humor will cause you to cry."

"I only laugh to keep from crying."

Noe hated being around "holy cops" like El Capitan and Salas. They didn't realize nobody gives a damn. You have to grab what you can while you can.

Jack and Jessie walked out the beach side of the Grand Palace, enjoying the sand and the surf. The water was a beautiful aqua, just like in the brochure.

The Grand Palace was in the elbow of the island. The old part of Cancun was on the mainland with a barrier island running for about fifteen miles along the coast. This was ideal for tourists and hotels. The Grand Palace was five miles down Kukulcan Boulevard. The barrier island must have had fifty hotels on it, and they all stayed busy. There was a police station near the hotel with the main station located in the center of the old downtown area.

Jessie and Jack walked in the white sand toward the police station without talking. It was a small building with twenty-some officers walking around, doing various "police" chores. The building seemed to have holding rooms, but no large confinement cell area. The clerk had them take a seat. The captain would see them, but only for a moment. He had another commitment.

Captain Joaquin Alejandro Sanchez greeted Jessie and Jack warmly. "Mr. Fitzgerald, welcome. What brings you out so early on a Sunday morning?"

"Good morning, Captain. I'm here to report that my daughter is missing. She didn't come home, and we wanted to know if you could help us."

"Yes, I know. We had a call about it yesterday from Ms. Broom. Please write down a description of your daughter and what she was wearing when she was last seen. If you have a photo of her, that would be good. Now if you'll excuse me, I have another commitment."

Jack was amazed at how callous the captain was. This was his only daughter. "Excuse me, Captain. My daughter is missing. She doesn't just go off like this. Something has happened to her! If you won't talk to me, then let me see the boss."

"I am the boss, Senor Fitzgerald, and you are rude. Please excuse me." With that, the captain walked out of the office and out of the building.

Jack couldn't remember the last time someone talked to him that way. "Jessie, go back to the hotel and wait for me there. Don't talk to anyone else about this. I'm going to follow the captain and make him help us."

Jack spun around and headed out of the building as well. The captain never turned around but kept walking straight toward the beach. There in a café on the beach, he embraced a beautiful Hispanic woman. She kissed him on one cheek and then the other. She was tall with dark hair, and as she looked his way, she smiled. Her smock hung loosely over her nicely shaped figure. Jack found himself staring at her. Then she and the captain took their seats.

A secret meeting with a girlfriend was more important than finding out what happened to his Sara. Jack entered the café with fire in his eyes. "Captain, you don't have time to meet with me about my daughter because you're meeting with your girlfriend? Does your wife know about her? I assume you are not his wife? Am I right?" Jack unleashed his anger on two people who deserved maybe even worse.

The captain had planned for Mr. Fitzgerald to follow him, but his manners were not acceptable under any circumstance. "Mr. Fitzgerald, I will forgive your rudeness and attribute it to the loss of someone special. However, don't push me. Please sit down. Senor Fitzgerald, it is my pleasure to introduce you to Senora Santos." Both nodded to each other.

"Senora Santos also lost a daughter two nights ago. Senor Fitzgerald, I did not talk with you at the station because the walls have ears. My office is not a safe place to discuss sensitive information. My men are paid very little. Those who seek information can buy it easily. I have two men I trust, and they are working on the two missing girls. Her friend Jessie called us last night. If you are here, then my men will think that this is a very special case, and it will draw attention to it. If you want to help, get on a plane and fly back to New York City. Let me do my job without you making it harder."

Jack felt terrible for his words. Across him sat one of the prettiest women he had ever seen. Her beauty contrasted with her obvious grief. Jack spoke to the captain, but his eyes didn't leave Senora Santos. "I'm sorry for not understanding and for my behavior. I'll go back to New York, but can't you tell me what you know?"

"Senor, you are working out of emotion. I cannot tell you what I know because you will go and check it out and blow all of our work. Just go back to New York and let me do my job."

"I believe you, Captain, but I'm going to look around Cancun some. I won't ask anyone else questions, but I need to know what's here. Do you think she was murdered?"

"Senor, there were no unclaimed bodies after this weekend. Please go back tonight."

"I will go back soon."

The captain handed Jack his personal card. "If you have any questions, call me at this number. Only about twenty people have this number. It should be safe."

"Senora Santos and Captain, thank you for your time." With a nod to both, Jack left the café feeling a bit like a cad, but he felt better about his daughter's case. He walked back toward the Grand Palace. It was time to talk to Jessie about every detail she could remember.

As Jack walked back to the hotel, he was no longer a raging bull. The beach area was beautiful. The shops were busy with tourists buying that special item that would get put on a shelf or in a drawer. Jack stopped and took off his shoes. He bought a cup of coffee and just sat down on the cabana's lounge chair, looking out at the surf. The Grand Palace was a beautiful hotel located in a perfect setting. The aqua-colored water beat against the white sand. How wonderful it all was.

His house was on the waterfront in Glen Cove, but he never just sat down and watched the surf. Along with giving his family more time, he would start giving himself more time. He needed to sit and watch the surf at his place. The pool was mostly decoration for Jack. The kids loved it, but Jack never had time to enjoy it. He was always going somewhere or always had something else to do. His eyes closed, and he slept.

Two hours later, Jessie found Jack asleep in his chair. "Uncle Jack, are you okay?"

"I'm sorry, Jessie. I must have dozed off. What time is it?"

"It's almost noon, and I'm starving."

"Good. I want you to eat and then get on a plane back to New York."

"What about you? Aren't you coming with me?"

"No. I think I'll stay and look around a bit. I am going to need you to tell me what you girls did. You know, what tours you went on. I'm going to need every name that you can remember. Did anyone look suspicious? Those kinds of things, and then I'll put you on a plane and you're out of here. Remember, you have to pick up your class schedule tomorrow."

"Uncle Jack, I want to stay here with you. I can tell you more as we go around."

"I know, honey, but you need to go home. Your parents are going to want to see you."

Jessie started crying. "I know all of that, but it doesn't feel right leaving without Sara. How can I go home without her? You aren't."

"There's a lot of truth in what you're saying, but probably I'll be returning without Sara also. It breaks my heart to send you home, but I can't take a chance on making someone angry and causing them to hurt you. I won't stay long, and then I'll be by to visit with you, you know, to see if you've remembered anything else. When something comes to mind, be sure to write it down right then. Okay?"

"Sure, Uncle Jack."

"What should we eat for lunch?"

"How about fajitas?"

"Sounds good to me. What are they?"

Later, after putting Jessie on the plane, Jack felt sick. He loved Jessie, but she was going home to her parents. No one could replace Sara. He hated to think about what his chances were of finding one young lady in such a large world.

There at the airport, he stopped and had a martini. It was time to call Victor and Kate and face the music. He would be staying awhile.

"Hello, Kate. I have only a little bit of news. We have no idea what happened to her. She hasn't turned up anywhere, if you know what I mean. She may have been kidnapped. I'm only basing it on a wild guess."

"What do you mean 'we'?"

"I mean I've spoken with the police captain, and he told me that another girl also turned up missing Saturday. I can only speak for Sara. I don't think she would have just taken off or done something crazy."

"I agree with you, Jack. When does your flight come in?" There was silence for only about seven seconds, but it seemed like several minutes. "Jack, you're not thinking of staying down there?"

"Kate, I'm going to look around. I'm not going to do anything crazy or risky. The police captain tried to convince me not to, but I can't come home yet. If you want to come on down for a couple of days, Julie would probably stay in the house with Jere."

"I'm not leaving Jere at a time like this. I don't know how you can still be down there when your family is up here going through what we are going through."

"Kate, I'm here doing what I think I need to be doing. I'll call you in a couple of days." He knew there was no answer that was going to make Kate feel better. Her only daughter had just disappeared. Still, he didn't feel good himself.

Now it was time to check in on the business. "Hello, Victor."

"How ya doin', Jack?"

"Not good. I need another martini." Jack just held up his glass, and the bartender nodded.

"I mean did you find out anything?"

"The short answer is no. I'm not going to talk much about this over a phone. They could be tapped. I'm going to stay down here for a week. Clear my calendar of everything that you can. You, Frank, and Kate will have to cover those other things. I'm simply in the right place here. I need to figure some things out. Victor, I'm only thinking out loud now, so don't panic. I might sell my shares in the company and step aside."

"Wow, Jack. Stop and think about what you're saying. Take a week off, but don't get out. This didn't happen because you were successful."

"I know, but I didn't know Sara well enough to lose her, Victor. I should have been at home more. I'm not going to make that mistake with Jere. I was a great provider, but I'm not sure how good a dad I was. Don't tell anyone what I've told you. I'm not going to do anything quickly, other than stay here. You know what else I want you to do for me?"

"I guess you probably want me to go by the apartment and get you some clothes and stuff."

"Americana South will fly it down. Log it under the name of Jack Allen. I need to drop the Fitzgerald for now. In the hotel, I'll be registered under Jack Allen. That means I'll need some cash. You know I have about thirty in the safe. Send all of it with the pilot and a lockbox. Thanks, Victor."

"You're welcome. Jack, be safe."

From the airport, Jack took a taxi back to the hotel. There he met with the manager and shared some of his plan. His suitcases would arrive with the evening flight from New York, and at that time, he would register as Jack Allen. He no longer wanted people to know Mr. Fitzgerald was still in town.

Onboard the *Verdi Mare*, Rick hadn't given the girls any more drugs. He wanted them to start withdrawing from the drugs he had given them. He wanted them in the pink of health when they arrived on Balta.

Ronnie awoke to a room that was slightly moving. In the room with her was a blonde, probably about her age. They were dressed alike, wearing tank tops and cutoffs. Someone had changed their clothes.

The blonde was still drugged. Ronnie moved to get off the bed and decided she needed to throw up. Veronica Maria Santos didn't know how long she'd been sleeping or where she was. It was time to wake up Ms. Gringo.

"Hey. Wake up. You need to wake up."

Sara opened her eyes to a spinning room. She, too, felt the room moving. Before she could talk, she had to find a bathroom or can. Sara lost whatever was in her stomach. Holding on to the toilet bowl didn't stop the room from moving, but she spoke. "Who are you, and where are we?"

"I don't know. I thought maybe you could tell me."

"I'm Sara from New York."

"Hi. I'm Ronnie. I am from Cancun. How'd we get here?"

Shaking her head as if to say *I don't know*, she said, "Try the door."

Ronnie moved slowly to the door. It was locked.

"Please don't scream. My head can't take it. We were drugged and brought here. They are not going to let us out."

"Sara, de Nuevo York. How can you be so calm?" Ronnie could speak perfect English, but the drug was messing her speech up.

Sara responded with a mocking tone, "Ronnie from Cancun, I'm not calm. I'm sick." Sara lost a little more from her stomach. She steadied herself by holding on to the toilet. "I think this toilet is moving."

"I think we are on a boat, a very big boat."

Jere was supposed to start school in a couple of days, but his sister was missing in Cancun. He was a senior, and this was supposed to be his year to have fun. How would he be able to do that with Sara missing?

With her car keys in hand, Kate was ready to get her chores underway. The first one was to get Jere some new school clothes that were acceptable to him and her. Neither wanted to go, but Kate knew school would start in two days and this had to be done today. "Come on, Jere. We've got to get going."

"Mom. I don't feel like buying clothes right now."

"Jere, I don't feel like taking you right now, but school starts on Wednesday and we need to get some things."

"Yeah." Jere walked like he was going to meet the ugliest girl in the world, slowly, one foot in front of the other. Finally, he made it to the door. "What do you think happened to Sara?"

"Jere, I'm sure I have no idea." She thought saying it might somehow make it happen. Kate had decided not to think about it. When she found out, then she would deal with reality, not wonder.

"When is Dad coming home?"

This made her angry. How could he dare to stay over in Cancun? He needed to be here with his family. He was only wasting his time down there. If he thinks anything else, then that is just foolish bullshit. "I don't know. I'd guess Friday."

"Mom. Don't be mad at Dad. He just has to look some. He's not going to find Sara, but he has to look."

"Well, he should be home and let the professionals look. What happens to us if he gets into trouble? He doesn't belong there. He needs to be here, damn it!"

Jere wasn't ready for his mom to beat up on his dad. He loved them both, but they seemed to argue a lot. He refused to get on either side. "Let's go get my clothes, Mom."

Jack had his fourth martini of the day. Cancun was too big to see in one day. He thought he'd have to get an early start tomorrow. He wanted to visit the club where Sara was last seen. He didn't really think he would find anything, but he just needed to go there. The captain said that she left the Spirit Club with a young man, and that was the last time she was seen.

Monday,
SEPTEMBER 4, 2000

Martinis work pretty well as sleeping aids. Jack woke up around nine but didn't get up until ten. For now, he was Jack Allen. He did have a nice room on the beach side of the Grand Palace. The irony of the situation was that this might have been the nicest place he had ever visited, but he was visiting it because Sara hadn't come home. He knew Kate would never come back, but maybe Jere would come down here with him for a visit.

After a shower and shave, Jack hired a taxi to give him a tour. Except for conquering Spaniards and hurricanes, he felt that Cancun was an Eden. By the end of the day, he didn't feel better; he just felt tired. He took another shower and then a nap.

A knock on the door broke into his dream. He didn't remember the dream, other than that he was running after someone. His shirt was damp from the dream. His body thought he really had been running. Another knock helped him roll out of bed. He slipped on his hotel robe and checked to see who might be at his door.

"Excuse me for bothering you, Mr. Allen, but the airlines found your suitcase and your box."

"Thank you." Jack signed for the suitcase and money box.

Police Lieutenant Noe Diaz was a great cop who graduated at the top of his class. His university scores were almost a perfect 4.0. Criminals were afraid of him. His only problem was that he, too, was a criminal. In the world of crime, he had climbed the ladder of success by being meaner and nastier than anyone he confronted. His only bit of conscience sat in the captain's office. Captain Sanchez knew Diaz for the dirt he was, and that bothered Diaz. He would be captain one day, and Sanchez would be dead.

Noe wanted to know more about the two missing girls. Surely he could make some money from their absences. The problem was that nobody knew anything. He would have to get the information from the captain. "Capitan, tell me about these two girls that are missing."

The only thing Captain Sanchez was going to give him was grief. "So now, Lieutenant Diaz, you are giving orders to me again. We've talked about this. You are the lieutenant, and I'm El Capitan. You don't give me orders."

"There you go, changing the subject. I just want to help."

"If you just want to help, then go resign."

"Why don't you like me, Captain? I am a hard worker."

"Diaz, you do work hard, but only for Diaz. Lieutenant Rogelio was a good policeman, and you had him taken out. When I can prove that, I will turn the key that will lock you up with your friends for the rest of your life. Now get out of my face and try to act like a policeman."

Noe was seething, but he wouldn't let the captain know. His days were numbered, and the number was getting smaller. He still hadn't found out what he wanted to know. The captain only tried to solve the cases. Noe tried to make money from solving the cases. If traffic cops were taking bribes, he wanted some of their bribe. With drug traffickers, he wanted their dirty money and the drugs as well. If two girls were missing, he wanted to know how he could profit from it. He didn't care about the girls. He only cared about how he could profit from their case.

Jack had put off visiting the Spirit Club until after supper. Then he made himself go. He walked into the Spirit Club feeling like a minor out on the town for the first time. There were butterflies in his stomach, and he felt very guilty. Kate was at home with Jere, and he was alone in a bar in Cancun. Most places he went, people would try to get his attention and he could never be alone. Now he felt more alone than he could ever remember.

As he entered, he began looking around and mentally mapping the place. This was the last place anyone had seen Sara. That thought almost made him throw up. He stopped himself, with his hand going to his mouth. The quick motion made him wobble a little. He felt alone and lost, and his daughter had been taken from this place. Depression swirled up around him, and he had trouble breathing.

Laura walked up from behind him and handed him her drink. "Here, take this. You know that the capitan is not going to be happy with us for coming here tonight." With her Mexican accent, she stretched out her words, trying to be understood.

Startled, Jack looked at her, not knowing what was happening. "What are you giving me?"

Laura was normally passive, but she looked into this tall gringo's blue eyes and knew he needed a friend, here and now. "Does it matter?"

Overwhelmed with depression, Jack was virtually speechless. "Not really. What are you doing here?" In a swift motion, he downed the contents of her glass.

"You have to ask?" Her face said, *Come on, Jack. I lost a daughter also.* "Come. I'm sitting over here. You walked past me just now."

Jack's eyes filled with tears. His hand came back to his face as he whispered, "Are you as depressed as I am?" He couldn't believe he was sharing his innermost thoughts with a woman whose name he could barely remember. This was not the old stone-faced Jack of the past.

"Probably more." She didn't say he was a nice distraction. She just kept looking into his blue eyes.

"Then we make a good couple. Life was so good, and then all of a sudden, you're lying on the floor, wondering how you got there. I'm having trouble breathing because my daughter is missing." Looking down and shaking his head, he said, "What could I have been thinking about, letting her come down here alone?"

"Senor Fitzgerald, you cannot change the past. You must look at the future."

"I'm not Fitzgerald now. I'm going by Jack Allen. Call me Jack."

Laura had motioned for two more of the same drink. She handed one to Jack. He seemed to relax a little. They sipped on their drinks, and they refilled them again and again. He and Laura watched and talked into the early morning hours. They saw many things—men hitting on women and women hitting on men. They saw the young acting old and the old acting young. They saw people trying to escape life from where they had come. It seemed to be working, at least for this one night. The music and dance were lively, and many were laughing and having a great time.

At 1:30, two bartenders hopped up on the bar and started dancing. Soon others joined in, and clothes started coming off. Laura and Jack looked at each other and decided to leave without saying a word. Outside, Jack offered to drive Laura anywhere she wanted to go.

"Can I drop you somewhere?"

"Thank you. No. I can take the bus. Number 17 goes right by my place. Where are you staying? I can give you a call tomorrow. I mean today."

"I'm at the Grand Palace."

"Yes. I know this place. It's nice. *Buenos noches.*"

"Good night." Tonight Jack's smile was real. So many times in his line of work, he would flash his smile, but it was just good business. Laura had helped ease his loss. He thought that so often people say they understand a situation when they have no clue. Laura had lost a daughter, and she knew. Jack was able to say what he really thought for the first time in a long time. They had talked about how their girls were now and when they were little.

When he laid his head on his pillow, he was still smiling. Sometimes you feel like you are doing the right thing, but there is no way to justify it. He knew being here in Cancun and looking for his daughter was the right thing to do. Soon he would have to leave, but if nothing turned up, he would return and look for his little girl.

For Jack, the night had been too short. The ringing of the phone broke into his dream.

"Good morning, Mr. Allen. Will you take a phone call from a Ms. Laura Santos?"

"Yes."

"One moment, sir."

"Hello."

"Hi. Did I disturb you?"

"No. I was just lying here, relaxing."

"I called to see if you wanted to get something to eat together. I enjoyed our time together last night and wanted to visit some more."

"Do you want to come here, or shall I meet you somewhere else?"

"I will go there. I will look for you in the lobby. Okay?"

"Do I say *si*?"

"You could. *Bueno* means 'okay.'"

"*Bueno.*"

Jack seldom did things he liked. Most everything he did revolved around keeping or making more money. Most all his meetings were necessary. This time, he was going to meet with someone because he really felt good being with her. His mind wasn't on sex, but Laura was beautiful. They were meeting just to talk and relax. Jack decided there needed to be more talking and relaxing in his life. The new Jack's life was developing a new list of rules. Spend a lot of time with Kate and Jere. Enjoy the day. Enjoy his house. And now, spend more time talking and relaxing with people he enjoyed being with. The business was getting pushed further down the list of those things that were now important to him.

Laura walked up to Jack and kissed him on the cheek, as was the Mexican custom. Jack smiled and thought he could get used to this. They had a table waiting for them on the ocean side. The ocean breeze could be strong at times, but today it was mild. The coffee was stronger than Jack was used to, but not too strong. Again they talked on into the afternoon. Jack felt at peace and was really relaxing.

"Jack, I need to run some errands, but I will let you buy me dinner and a dance later at the Spirit Club."

"I think I can deal with that." She had said what Jack had wanted to say, but he didn't know if he was being too pushy.

"Meet me at Margarita's at seven."

"Bueno."

She kissed his cheek again and was gone. Jack didn't go anywhere. He was enjoying the moment. Her perfume lingered after she had left, and he liked it. The kiss, the brush of cheeks, and a calm peace inside. The waves crashed onto the beach. The birds talked to each other about where their next bite was coming from. The breeze was just enough. He stayed right there, sipping on a bottle of water, enjoying the ocean, and relaxing more. Again the corporation was sliding further down his list of priorities.

Later in the afternoon, Jack took $10,000 in cash with him to visit a certain police captain. The captain was glad Jack really was leaving the next day. They went for a short walk to get out of the office and away from walls that might have ears.

"Captain Sanchez, I need you to take this newspaper and use the contents to buy any information you might need to purchase."

"How do you know you can trust me, Jack?"

"I've made a lot of money deciding on whom to trust. I think you're a good bet. If you ever need a job, give me a call first."

"You are very kind, Senor. Now get out of town." He laughed.

"Si, El Capitan."

At seven, Jack walked into Margarita's. A smile came back to a face that hadn't smiled much recently. Then he saw one of the most beautiful women he had ever seen. Laura was dressed to kill. Never mind her long black dress. Just her black hair, the dark eyeliner highlighting her big brown eyes, and her red sensuous lips were enough to make all the men in the restaurant take notice. Jack had enjoyed her friendship and company as they shared their grief together. But tonight Laura was the sexiest and prettiest woman in the place, and she was with him. He just stood there looking at her, so she came up to him and kissed him on the cheek. She was very pleased with his reaction. It was more than she had hoped for.

"Is something the matter, Jack?" She smiled teasingly.

"Actually, something is right. You look beautiful tonight."

"Good, because it cost me a lot of money." Her smile widened as she saw Jack looking only at her. It had been a long time since a man had looked only at her.

"I haven't felt like dressing up in a long time. I have been busy being a mother. There was no time or money to dress up. Jack, you've helped me feel better about myself. Life was rushing along, and then my world stopped when Ronnie didn't come home. I knew something terrible had happened to her. I need her to come home. Our talking has helped me.

You have helped me. I know that you are going home tomorrow, so I dressed up for you. I just wanted you to remember a happy, pretty Laura Santos."

"You've spent your money well." Now they were both smiling and enjoying the moment. Jack hadn't noticed, but he was holding Laura's hand. He led her to their table. Again they talked. Tonight it was about life in New York.

"Tell me what you do."

"I have a business that will invest your money and make money for both of us."

"Let me see. People give you their money and tell you to invest it for them?"

"Yes. They pay me to take their money. Then I buy into companies that I like and wait for them to make money."

"Do you own many companies?"

"I'm the majority owner of my company. The others we just invest in and let them run them."

"Are you good at making money with money people give you?"

"I have worked very hard at making money and am good at it. Then I confused making money with living. My wife, Kate, and I have two great kids, but I was still wrapped up in making more money. People told me how good I was at it, and I liked that. Kate liked it. She got her dream home. It bought me a lot of things, and I liked that. But I'd give it all back for one more hour with Sara. When she left, I didn't know I'd never see her again." His eyes filled with tears as he revealed words that weren't supposed to come out.

Laura took Jack's hand and then embraced him. Laura had tears in her eyes as well. Their food came, and they ate quietly for a few minutes. Then Laura waved over the mariachi, and they played some lively Mexican music. At first, it made Jack uneasy. After a couple of songs, he started liking the music. He enjoyed the restaurant and the Mexican food. He enjoyed his Mexican host the most.

As they walked into the Spirit Club, Jack knew he needed that drink again. "What was that drink you gave me last night?"

"Sit down, I'll get us something."

It was unusual for anyone to give orders to the CEO, but he took them and sat. He thought he could get used to Cancun, Mexico, and Laura. Ronnie was lucky to have her for a mother. Laura brought her special drink, and they sipped and talked. They talked on a level that Jack only spoke with Kate and his best friend, Victor. Lately, Kate and Jack hadn't really been talking. They lived together and went places together, but it was mechanical and cold. He made a note to talk more with Kate.

Jack and Laura talked a lot and danced a little. The dancing in the Spirit Club was, well, spirited. Jack thought it might take a little while to learn, but he liked dancing with Laura. They had a good time, and both were able to laugh.

One more time, when it was time to go, Laura took the bus home. She didn't want her friends and family asking questions about her date. Ronnie was still missing, and the focus should stay there. Laura also knew she had eaten with a married man, and breaking up a home was not in her plans. She would not see him again. She was too drawn to him. It was easy to understand how people could trust him with their money. *He has been through enough*, she thought to herself. Then she thought, How could she stay away? Tomorrow would take care of everything, because tomorrow a plane would take him back to New York.

Jack had liked being with Laura. Yes, they shared their grief, but a lot more. She was a classy lady. It also made Jack realize how much he missed Kate. Tomorrow a plane would take him back to New York and his family. He was ready to see his son as well. It was time to go home. He was more relaxed than he had been in a long time. When his head hit the pillow, he was asleep, smiling.

Jack flew in first class with Americana South, but only the pilot knew one of the owners was aboard. He was Mr. Allen returning from Cancun. He had decided not to bring the Fitzgerald jet down because it might let a lot of people know Sara Fitzgerald was missing. Jack sat in his very comfortable seat and was happy about his time in Cancun. He found out very little, but Cancun was no longer a mystery.

Victor was there to meet him, without Kate. Her absence said that she was not happy with his actions and that there would be more to pay.

"Hello, boss."

"Hi, Victor." He shook hands with one of his real friends. He was glad to see him. "No Kate?"

"I offered, but she said she had things to do."

"Don't worry. I've been in the doghouse before. It's just good to be home."

Often Tony drove Jack, and he was driving today. On the way home, Victor brought Jack up-to-date on Fitzgerald Group. The year 2000 looked to be their best year yet. Profits were up and climbing.

Tony pushed a button and a large metal gate opened and they pulled on through. The Fitzgerald home was a small estate. It was located in Glen Cove, just outside New York City. Jack knew he would enjoy the day and the estate. He would talk to Kate. Whether she would respond was another question.

Victor read his boss's expression and knew he was home for the day. "Will you be in tomorrow?"

"Yes, I'll have Tony bring me in around ten. See you then."

"Good luck." Victor smiled as he and Tony pulled away. He'd seen Kate angry before, and he was glad he wasn't staying.

Maged Kadir was Egyptian by birth, a father to three grown daughters. They were all in America now, with their mother and their new lives. His connections with the CIA had paid dividends. At six feet, he was tall for an Egyptian. His winning smile had served him well with the ladies and in business. He'd served in the military as an officer and then left after Sadat was murdered. Life led him out to sea, and after a few years, he found himself in charge of a large oil freighter. His captain had suddenly quit, and he was asked to take his place. Captain Ali Al Otaibi refused to do what Maged chose to do.

Ibrahim Al Balta was paying him $250,000 for this one trip. Maged was transporting two teenage girls who had parents somewhere that were going crazy. He was feeling very sorry for himself, but not sorry enough to let them go. Ibrahim would chase him down and kill him. So for now he had to live with the fact that he was trafficking white slaves.

Thus far, he had refused to look at them. Somehow he thought if he didn't look at them, maybe he didn't really have them.

At that moment, Rick walked into the helm. Rick worked directly for Ibrahim, taking orders only from him. It was Rick's job to select and care for the girls. "Rick, how are the passengers?"

"They are okay. Anka is taking very good care of them. But they aren't happy, and they want you to turn this tanker around and let them go."

"How do they know it's a tanker?"

"They aren't dumb. You know I only pick the best for Ibrahim."

"I don't know anything. And that's what I want to know—nothing." Rick was having a little fun with the captain now. "Let me describe them to you."

"No! And get off my bridge. I'm only concerned about their health."

"Don't get too concerned. Or I'll have to mention it to Ibrahim." Rick had made his point. The trouble was that he didn't like being around Ibrahim either. Ibrahim would kill you for nothing. If Rick reported the captain, Ibrahim might kill both of them. So Rick would not be reporting anything.

In their chambers below, Veronica and Sara were not moving around very much. The drugs that had been given to them had left them with splitting headaches, and the ship kept going up and down. It was slight, but the land-lovers didn't like it.

"Ronnie, how are you doing?"

"Probably about as good as you. I think we're withdrawing from the drugs they gave us the first few days."

"What's going to happen to us?"

"We've talked about this already. Rick got you, and Troy got me. They are probably both on this tanker, shipping us, as well as the oil."

"Well, at least we aren't dead. I want to think my dad will find us, but I know he won't. But I do know he'll try."

"At least you have a father. I just have my mother."

"Okay, when my father does find me, you can come."

"You're so kind." Veronica Santos was just your normal Mexican girl. She had just finished high school and was about to enter the university. In Mexico, she knew she would have to work hard to have a good life. She wasn't sure if she was going to stay in Mexico, but that decision could wait now—maybe for a long time.

Sara and Ronnie had been strangers, but they were becoming sisters. Life had borne them in different lands and with different economic backgrounds. On this ship, those differences meant nothing.

Sara started crying again. "Ronnie, what are we going to do?"

No words would help her. Ronnie just held her, and they slept again.

Maged looked at the three photos of his girls, and tears came to his eyes. What was he thinking? He should never have agreed to pick up those two girls. If someone took his girls, he would hunt the people down and kill them very slowly. What would the parents of these two do? Maged let the pictures of his daughters fall into the wastebasket. He could no longer look at his girls without thinking about his passengers. There were more pictures at home. He started to take out the white medicine but got his gin instead. Just a few more weeks of sailing and then he could drop off the girls. He would have to make at least one more trip before retiring. If he quit when they got back, Ibrahim would kill him.

Maggie couldn't believe her eyes. Mr. Fitzgerald was home during the daytime. She seldom ever saw him, but never during the day.

"Good morning, Mr. Fitzgerald."

"Good morning, Maggie. And I'm Jack."

"Yes, sir."

Jack didn't hear her. He was looking at his home. What a beautiful place. Kate had really made the most of it. When they did their talking, he thought he would mention it to her. Then he looked outside and took off.

"Sir. Would you like a cup of coffee? The paper?"

"Yes, Maggie. Bring both."

Maggie had never seen him act this way. He was a different person. He had the same voice and body, but he was acting really strange. Shaking her head, she went off to get this new boss the paper and some coffee.

Jack walked out past the pool to the beach area. The breeze was strong and smelled of the sea. He loved it. As in Cancun, the birds were discussing where to find the next bit of food. He stood there for a long moment, wondering why he hadn't done it before. He walked back up to the house and sat next to the pool. Now the shoes came off and the jacket and tie.

Maggie swapped the clothes and the newspaper. The coffee was on the table already.

As Maggie passed Mario, he asked, "What's Mr. Fitzgerald doing here during the day?"

"Oh, that's not Mr. Fitzgerald, that's Jack. I don't know what he's done with Mr. Fitzgerald."

Kate knew that Jack would come in and hug her and say how much he missed her, but she wasn't having any of it. She was so angry with him that she couldn't see straight. How could he have stayed down on the beach in Mexico while his family suffered back here? Kate had told a few friends Sara was missing, but not many. She really didn't want to talk about it until she had spoken with Jack, and he wouldn't come home. How could he stay there!

The gate opened for her, and she drove into their estate. She thought he would be sitting in the living room, waiting for her to come home. She was surprised when he wasn't. "Maggie, where's Mr. Fitzgerald?"

"Ma'am, he's out on the patio."

Jack had just dozed off but woke with the sound of Kate's walking. "Hi." He stood up to hug her but chose not to. Her scowl warned him to stay away.

"You chose to come home, finally. What were you thinking, Jack?"

"I guess I was thinking of me."

"You're damned right you were just thinking of you. She's my daughter too." Kate had been trying not to cry, but she started again.

Jack reached for her, but she held out her arm. "Stop. You weren't here earlier, and as far as I'm concerned, you're not here now." With those words came a spin and a quick departure. Kate went to the bedroom and locked the door.

Jack sat down and wondered if he deserved all that. He had had Laura to share his feelings with. He wondered who Kate had shared her grief with. He chose to go to the door and see if she would let him in. "Kate, I know I wasn't here for you, but I'm prepared to change that. Can I tell you what I found out?"

Kate had known this would happen, but she wasn't letting him off the hook that easily. He would need to stew for a while. Maybe she would talk to him after he returned from tomorrow's workday. "Check with me tomorrow."

"Okay." Jack knew they would play this "I'm upset" game, but he wasn't playing. He was living. She could be angry if she wanted to be, but he was not going to play along.

Jack returned to the kitchen to find out his son's schedule from Maggie. "Maggie, what time does Jere get home?"

She wasn't sure if it was Mr. Jack or just plain Jack, so she went with *sir*. "Sir, school lets out at three, but he's got football practice after that. I suppose Tony will go and get him then."

"No, I'll go and get him. What I need right now is for everyone to leave. Take the rest of today off and tomorrow."

"Jack, you want me to tell everyone to go?" Maggie couldn't believe what she was hearing.

"Yes. Sara didn't come back from Cancun, and she is missing. The police don't think she was murdered because there's no body, at least yet. My family just needs some time to be alone and grieve."

"Oh, sir. We couldn't leave you alone now! Sara was our little girl too!"

"The way you can help is by letting us be alone as a family."

"Yes, Jack. We'll go. I'm really sorry about Sara."

"This needs to be kept a secret, Maggie."

"Yes, sir. Bye." She hugged the new Jack and left with tears in her eyes. *This explains why he was acting so strange.*

Next Jack needed to check in with Victor. "Hi, Victor. Where are you?"

"It's two in the afternoon, boss. I'm at the office."

"It's time for me to take a week off like we discussed, Victor. My mind is not on work right now. I need you to reschedule things that I have to do. Everything else I want you and Frank to take care of. Frank can take care of the Group business, and you can take care of mine. Outside of the Group, I'm just taking a week's leave."

"I'm going to release to the staff that Sara is missing, okay?"

"Yes. But her life may depend on them keeping it a secret."

"I'll pass that on. Jack, you take care of your family, and we'll do all right. You've taught us pretty good."

"Thanks, friend. One more thing. When I come back, I don't want people passing their regrets. Tell them to just raise their right hand and give a little wave. It'll be our code."

"Got it. Bye."

Next Jack needed to go and pick up his son, but he had four hours to wait. Off came the clothes and into the pool he went. He couldn't remember the last time he had swum in his own pool. *Another item for the list: Swim more with my family.*

Kate soon tired of waiting for Jack to come back as she had expected him to. Hunger brought her out of her lair.

"Maggie." Of course, there was no answer. She said it a few more times.

On her wondering, she wound up at the pool. There was her husband, swimming nude.

"What the hell are you doing?" *How could he swim like that with the staff still here?*

"If you're only going to scream at me, then don't talk to me." He was relaxing and having a good time. She could be angry if she wanted to.

"Jack! Where are your clothes?" She was incredulous.

"You're standing next to them."

"I mean your suit. Jack, we have staff around here."

"Remember, you locked the door. I couldn't get to my swimsuit. Anyway, we don't have anyone else here. I sent them all home."

"Jack, what the hell's going on here?"

"I'm swimming, and you're screaming. You should stop screaming and jump in. It's more fun."

His crazy antics were distracting her from her anger. "I'm not jumping in there because it's in the middle of the day. We're outside. And, well, things will happen." She was blushing a little. Normally they didn't talk like this.

"The Kate I used to know twenty years ago would have jumped in already."

"That Kate is a mother of two grown children, and she doesn't behave like that anymore."

"What a shame."

Next came a big splash. She moved next to him, her hair dripping, but now a smile was on her face. "I still owe you some more screaming. You're not getting off this easy." Her smile grew larger as she fussed. Some of the anxiety she held deep inside while waiting for Jack to come home was released.

"Okay."

They kissed. He kissed her like they hadn't kissed in years. Her wet clothes came off, but Jack and Kate stayed in the pool. She was a beautiful woman. He paused a moment to admire her in the light.

Blushing a little, she asked, "What are you doing?"

"I'm looking at you. We make love, but it's always in the dark. You're beautiful."

"Oh, stop it. You're embarrassing me." But she didn't want him to stop.

He kissed her and then tasted her neck and went further. She loved his touch and always had. For Kate, there had been no other man. Still, Jack was her man. In the first few moments, she had been receiving, but now she started giving. Together they made passionate love.

After, she hung on to Jack. "Why didn't you come back?"

"I can't explain it so that it makes sense to you, but I had to look around. I didn't know what I'd find. Maybe I was waiting to see if her body would turn up. I visited the last place she was seen alive. I walked along the beach where she had walked with the girls. I don't know what I was looking for, but I didn't find it." What he thought but didn't say was that their Sara was now gone forever. Then he cried in big sobs, his large frame shaking.

Kate had never seen Jack cry in their twenty-three years together. She had seen him happy and sad, but she had never seen him cry. This dissipated her anger, and she held him. They cried together. Then they just held each other. He felt weak but good. He was sad, but he was with his wife and at home.

She knew he was feeling better and pushed him away. "I think you need to go pick up our son."

"Come with me, and we'll stop and eat at Pizza Hut."

"And I thought the day couldn't get any wackier."

In the garage, they had the choice of a two-seat Beamer, the big limo Tony drove them around in, or Sara's silver Beetle. Jack made another mental memo: *Get an SUV so the family could go places together.*

Ibrahim Al Balta knew his family had been pirates. Where exactly they had originated from he wasn't sure. He had seven sons and four daughters living on his island. They were the only family he knew he had. Pirating had gone out of fashion, and so the Al Balta family had started several businesses. They were covers for the pirating he was still doing. He had oil freighters carrying oil and other necessities for life. He had gotten into the ship-container business. Often his shipments included transporting weapons or drugs or diamonds. He kept an open mind but a very private pirate life.

Many nights he would sleep alone, not trusting anyone to be next to him while he slept. His wives had been loyal to a degree, but he chose not to find out how loyal. Now in his later years, he didn't sleep off the island. For him, the island was paradise and jail.

Anka, his favorite girl for now, had been gone for a couple of months now, onboard the *Verdi Mare*. She was to take care of the two new girls Maged was bringing. Ibrahim called the girls eye candy for his casino patrons. Ibrahim used to call his steady girl his wife, but he got tired of their claims on him. Now they were just his girls. Anka had been found in the Czech Republic. Ibrahim was convinced the Czechs had the prettiest ladies in the world. Anka was seventeen when she came to Al Balta Island. Roland had found her looking for life on the wild side. She pleaded with him to bring her to the island, and so he did. Roland seemed to forget to tell her about the one-way trip part. Anka lived for the here and now, and the here and now was living on Balta Island. Also, for now, she was the number one girl on the island. She liked the preferred treatment she received, but she knew it was only for a time.

Ibrahim told her two new girls were on their way here from Mexico. Anka knew they would be drugged. She had agreed to take the trip just to get off the island. Rick was her guard. This helped her keep life in perspective. No matter how she was treated on the island, she was a prisoner. Until it was time for her to leave, she would make the best of her situation. From time to time, she'd still use some drugs, but for her, they were always a choice.

Other young girls on the island found them to be a demon that controlled them, and eventually they died trying to get more. The island had everything, but everything had a price. You couldn't just have something. You had to come up with the money to have it. It didn't bother Ibrahim to snuff out their life. They were only an object to him. Like a pack of cigarettes, when he was finished with the product, he'd crush it.

Ibrahim had twenty girls working for him, and these girls never left the island. Two had tried recently, and that's why Maged was bringing two more. He didn't want the girls around if they weren't happy. It was bad for business to have unhappy girls around. But their fatal mistake was trying to escape. Now they were just part of the food chain in the sea.

Very few others stayed on the island. Workers would work shifts around the clock. Ferries ran every hour, but you had to have the right credentials or you might never be seen again. The casino compound was guarded better than most gold mines. The hotel connected to the casino, and they never closed.

On the back side of the island, Ibrahim ran his shipping business. The employees from the two organizations never mixed on the island. Security was tight for the shipping business, but it was also to keep the workers away from his casino. Ibrahim reported to no one, and only his people inspected the merchandise he was trading. His inspectors were very serious people, just like a civilian military. If someone was found with something that didn't belong to him, he would be beaten and then shot. There would be no trial or jail. The workers knew this, and so very little disappeared. After working for Ibrahim for five years, a worker could have his wages doubled, and doubled again in five more. Loyalty was rewarded by Ibrahim. Many workers stayed, and very few items turned up missing.

Jere was surprised his dad was home, but more surprised to see him in the VW. Jack got out and hugged his son. Normally, Jere didn't go in for public displays of affection, but his dad was home. It had only been four days, but it had seemed longer to Jere. "So what's the deal?"

"What do you mean, son?"

"So like, why are you and Mom driving around in Sara's bug?"

"We thought you might like to hit Pizza Hut."

"Cool. It's still a little weird."

Kate didn't say what she was thinking, but if Jere only knew.

At Pizza Hut, Jere couldn't wait to find out about Sara. "So what'd you find out, Dad?"

"The short answer is nothing. There is another girl missing as well. No bodies have gone unclaimed, and that's good. But we have no idea what's happened."

"So why'd you stay gone so long?"

Kate saw a chance to stick a little pin in. "My point too, Jere."

"I know where I was. Why? I hate to talk about it. I thought she might turn up, one way or another." Jack thought he needed one of those drinks Laura had gotten for him. He should have gotten the name of the drink at least.

"What, Dad?"

"There are no good options when it comes to Sara. Either she's been murdered or she's been kidnapped. I hope she's alive. We haven't received any contact for a ransom. So that would make her a white slave somewhere. If that's true, we have no clues. Zero."

There was a silence at the table now that was uncomfortable. Gus saved the day by bringing their pizza.

"Gus, can I get a beer?"

"Sure, sir. Miller okay?"

"Yes."

Jere chimed in, "Can you make it two, Gus?"

Kate was quick with "One will do just fine, Gus."

"But, Mom, I don't want to share Dad's."

"Don't worry, you won't have to. Jere and I'll have a coke."

Thursday,
SEPTEMBER 7, 2000

Kate was afraid to ask Jack why he wasn't getting up. "Jack, don't you need to be going somewhere?"

"Nope. I've got the week off."

"Who gave you the week off?"

"I did."

"You gave yourself last week off."

"This is still part of that week. Besides, I can be a good boss."

"Won't you be missed?"

"Yes and no. Yes, they'll miss me, but they'll have Frank telling them what to do and making decisions."

"Aren't you supposed to be doing that?"

"A week ago, I would have agreed with you. Then Sara turned up missing. Now I'm not even sure if I want to do this kind of work anymore."

"You can't quit!"

"A week ago, I would have agreed with you. Then Sara turned up missing. Work's not as important as family. I'd forgotten that. From now on, family comes first."

"Good. Now go to work."

"We're in the same room, but you aren't listening to me. I don't want to do this kind of work anymore."

"What will we do? How will we get by?"

"Kate, we are worth almost a billion. There's plenty of money."

"But I like going to your parties."

"You always fussed about going."

"That was just so you'd owe me. I could get you to do things for me. I don't want you to retire."

"Kate, I'm not retiring. I'm taking a week off to think about what I want to do for the rest of my life. I'm fifty-one, and I've been doing this sort of work for thirty years. I've had my own company the last fifteen. I'm responsible for twenty-two billion dollars. I'm tired of these golden handcuffs. I don't think I want to do this for another thirty. Right now, you're at the top of my list. Then Sara and Jere come next. I want to spend time with my family. I want to travel some. I want to sit and watch the surf or read a book."

Kate was silent, but the battle wasn't over. She wasn't giving up her lifestyle that easily. Jack Fitzgerald had better get ready for a fight. Retiring meant losing the prestige she had when she was with Jack. She lay back down. It felt like she was now losing her husband along with Sara.

Later in the morning, Jack called the FBI to tell them his daughter was missing. They agreed to send out two agents to the estate. They stayed for about an hour and were polite, but Cancun was a Mexican problem. One agent turned back and said, "I'm not supposed to do this, Mr. Fitzgerald, but call this office. Johnny used to be a Jersey cop, but now he's the head of his own detective agency. I'd trust him with my daughter's life. I don't know if he'll find anything, but he can go where we can't."

Jack put the card in his pocket. He wasn't sure he wanted to hire a detective.

Kate grew very quiet and began staying away from Jack and Jere. At night, she'd just go to sleep. She refused his efforts at talking and at intimacy. At social events, she put on a good face.

Thursday,
SEPTEMBER 14, 2000

A week later, Jack reluctantly called Johnny, and they met.

"Before we talk about me, I'd like to talk about you. Tell me why you're not a cop any longer."

"I'd been a cop for twenty-five years and knew that it was time to get out. The bad guys had us, the good guys, jumping through hoops, while they sat back and laughed. I got to the point where I didn't jump when the captain said 'jump.' On that day, I decided I wasn't going to play by their rules any longer. So I left. I'm still interested in catching the bad guys, but now I play by their rules."

"How would you go about looking for a lost girl in Cancun?"

"I would need to make a trip down there. Stay there awhile and develop some contacts and see where things lead. I suppose you have an honest cop you're working with down there?"

"I trust Captain Sanchez, but not some of his coworkers. But they haven't found out anything. I don't want the trail to get too cold. I need to know what has happened to my little girl. If she's dead, I'd like to know who did it and how. If she's been kidnapped, then I want to know where and what can be done about it."

"I checked you out and I know that you can afford me, so I'm ready to take your case if you say the word."

"I'd like to talk it over with my wife."

"Sure."

Kate would hardly talk to Jack about it. She just made some noises and muttered. Jack decided without her help. He called Johnny back and turned him loose.

"You called, boss." Christi Douglas and Johnny Trudle had worked together as Jersey City police officers until about eighteen months ago. When he walked, she soon followed.

"Yes, and I'm not 'boss.' I'm 'darling.'"

"Sorry. You already have a wife."

"We have a new case. Sara Fitzgerald went to Cancun and didn't come back. Our expenses are being picked up by Dad to go down and investigate. Can you leave tomorrow?"

"If you're my husband, then you've got the couch."

"We'll be staying at the Grand Palace, and we have a suite reserved for us. That means you have your room and I have mine."

Johnny had used the number the captain had given Jack, so the three of them met privately, away from the police station. Nothing new had turned up, so Christi and Johnny spent several evenings drinking and dancing at the Spirit Club before returning to New York and Jack.

"Jack, there were no new clues. No bodies, nothing. We were at the Spirit Club several nights, and it just seemed like a normal club. I doubt it's involved. The owner is in his seventies and is looking to sell. That's not public, the manager said he was looking for a new job."

"Johnny, go down there and make your best deal and buy it. I'm not ready for it to become a parking lot. Victor and my accountant will go with you. Victor will need to be the CEO of the company buying it." A plan began forming in Jack's head. He had been wanting to go back to Cancun and just kind of wait around until something was found out. Maybe he could help find something out by running the Spirit Club.

"Jack, what's the name of Victor's company?"

They were meeting on his patio. The sea breeze was nice, and the sun wasn't too hot. It was a beautiful day. If he only had a name for his new company. The Sea something. His Expedition sat in the driveway. *The New York Sea Expedition Company.* "Its name is the New York Sea Expedition Company (NYSEC)."

"I've not heard of that one, Jack."

"Well, it doesn't exist yet, but it will before you take off in its corporate jet tomorrow. Christi, should I tell Victor to expect you as well?"

"Why not?" She was laughing at the idea of setting up a corporation in one day. It couldn't be done, but you can't tell that to these rich clients.

Johnny and Christi were told to meet Victor in front of Terminal 1 at JFK. Right on time, a big limo pulled up to the sidewalk where they were standing. On the side of the limo were the letters *N YSEC.* Tony got out and opened the door for them. They weren't sure what to do, but they got in. He placed their bags in the trunk.

"Good morning. I'm Victor Madden, and I work for Jack. We want people to see this car and jet with our logo on it. That's why you were picked up here."

"The logo is on the jet too?"

"It might be drying on the way to Cancun, but it's on there. This is Robert Bell, books, and Kim Doming is Jack's secretary."

Johnny introduced his partner. "And this is Christi, my coworker and wife for this trip."

With that, they were at the jet and ready to board. "What about clearing customs?"

"You did. Don't you remember?"

Life was different when you had a corporate jet and lots of money. Johnny thought he could get used to it.

The tanker had been in port for a day before Anka came back to check on the girls. "I'm supposed to show you to your quarters."

The girls didn't move. They just looked at Anka. Ronnie spoke, "If we don't go with you?"

"We discussed this at length on the way. Mr. Balta has twenty girls that he has brought here to work in his casino. We are captives on an island that he owns. If you don't come with me now, then he'll just drug you again. Then you will be brought to your rooms. If you don't resist, then you'll be free on the island. So please come with me."

With a nod to each other, the girls figured they didn't have an option. "Okay."

Anka continued her orientation. "We're on the shipping side of the island. The resort is on the other side. Ibrahim has us doing various jobs at the casino."

A limo pulled up and picked up the three ladies. Within minutes, they passed the casino and hotel. Then there was another gated entry, and they drove into their compound. The walls were high, and they had that razor wire at the top. The girls had just entered their prison.

For the three weeks onboard the tanker, their lives had been their own. That changed as they entered their "dorm." There were glass and cameras everywhere. They knew they were being watched as they moved closer to their rooms. They shared a small apartment with private bedrooms.

"Please wait here. A doctor will come here and give you both physicals. Please don't resist."

"You're a prisoner here, and you don't mind?"

"I do mind, but you can't do anything about it. If you resist, you can die. You two are replacing two that tried to escape."

Just then, a female doctor came in. "Ladies. Please remove your clothes." Anka had disappeared. Sara had a ton of questions to ask her. The next twenty-four hours for Sara and Ronnie were filled with tests and getting settled into their apartment. Again drained, they just slept on the sofa together.

Monday,
OCTOBER 2, 2000

Jack picked up Jere every evening after school. He was at every school event, even coming in to tutor sometimes. He made friends with some of the other football parents. He was liking his new life.

Kate only went to one game and then had to stay away after that. She saw her Jack changing, and she knew where it was going. Jack had stopped all nighttime activities. They no longer went to concerts or operas. Kate was becoming a real stay-at-home mom, and she didn't like it. She liked being the wife of a super CEO, owner of his own company.

Jack only worked half days now. The machine was well-oiled. Frank Burbon was pretty much running everything now. Frank was CEO and only reporting to Jack. Everything had to go through Frank. The exception was Jack's own staff. Victor and Kim stayed in touch with Jack. It wasn't official yet, but Jack had turned the company over to Frank and he was doing great.

Jere was doing great at his position as a defensive end. But his sister was still missing. Jack had become a dad involved with his son's school life. Some teens might have pushed their father away, but Jere needed his dad to be Dad. He needed a rock to lean on when there were no answers to his questions. His dad wasn't his buddy, he was Dad.

J ack and Jere returned from one of his football games. Jere hit the shower, while Jack sat on the couch. He sat there with his head down, not looking anywhere.

"What is it, Jack?"

"I can't do this anymore, Kate. I'm going to sell my part of the company. I've spoken with Frank, and he'll take my job. He's been doing it now for two months anyway."

"There's nothing I can do to change your mind?"

"No."

"Then I want a divorce."

Jack's head popped up, and his eyes widened. He knew it had been a possibility, but he had hoped it wouldn't happen.

Kate had planned her speech for a while. It came coldly. "I want half of the company stock, and I don't want you to sell my part. I want this house just like it is, and I want the New York apartment. I want all of the vehicles except your Expedition. Jere can drive the bug unless he chooses not to. And I want you to leave my house now, tonight. You can get your things some other time."

Jack was devastated. He just sat there.

Jere walked into the coldness of the room, looking at each parent. "What just happened here?"

"Your father and I are parting company. He's just about to leave."

Jere knew that his mom had pulled away, but he was shocked by the news. "No, Mom! You can't do this!"

"It's already done. Good night, Jack."

Jere looked at his father, his eyes pleading. He held his hands out. "Dad! You can't let her do this!"

Jack knew now that there was no going back. He wanted Jere to stay the night with his mom until he could figure out what to do, but she would not be taking Jere out of his life. "I'll be picking you up every morning for school. Good night." With his head bowed, he headed for the door.

"You can see your son as much as you like, just not me." Kate was like a statue, not showing any feeling, even to her son.

"Dad, don't leave me. I want to go with you!"

These words were ripping out Jack's heart. He wanted to take Jere with him, but he didn't know where he was going. "Jere, this is your home. I don't know where I'm sleeping at tonight. Stay here, and I'll see you in the morning."

A rage came over Jere that he'd never known before. He turned to the one causing the ache inside and pointed a finger at her. "You're not my mother! I hate you! I hate you! You can't do this to our family!"

Now Jack was screaming at his son. "Jere! Don't talk like that to your mother. She's been a great mother, and I'll not have you talking to her that way. Do you hear me!"

"Yes, I hear you!" Then he went to his room and slammed the door as hard as he possibly could. Speaking to no one, he said, "They can act like idiots, but if I get mad, it's disrespectful. Bullshit!"

Jack also left the room, but slowly and quietly.

Kate didn't leave the room. She sat down on the sofa and cried because her old life had just died. Jere's words burned her very soul. She had no idea he would take it so hard. He hated her. She told herself that it wouldn't last. But she really didn't know.

Jack made it to the Expedition and then collapsed. His wife of twenty-four years was really divorcing him. His daughter was missing, but he knew where to find his son. The money and power still held his wife. He couldn't be angry with her because he was there just a few months ago. She would have to figure out what she wanted. *Now,* he thought, *where to sleep?* His mind wouldn't work. It was as if a great fog had just moved in. His hands came to his face, and large sobs poured from the very depths of his soul.

K ate hadn't slept much during the night, but you couldn't tell. She was very attractive and ready to convince Frank that he needed to give her a job in her own company. She walked into Fitzgerald Group and found Frank Burbon, the new CEO. He was a tall man with wavy gray hair, looking every bit the part of CEO. He'd been with Jack for more than ten years and owned 20 percent of the company. "Good morning, Frank."

"Good morning, Kate. What brings you down here on a Saturday morning?"

"I'm going to work for you, at least for now."

"Excuse me. You seem to know something I don't."

"We are not selling all of our shares. Jack is selling his. I'm keeping mine. That makes me a majority owner. I don't want your job, but I do want a job and a nice title and Jack's old office."

"You sure give a lot of orders to the boss."

"We both know that Jack has made you the CEO. That's because he wants to get out of the business. I don't. Jack and I have parted company. He's not living with me any longer. So do you have a problem with what I just said?"

"All right. You can start work next week. Do you want me to hire you a secretary, or do you want to pick one for yourself?"

"What about Jack's?"

"She's going with him, and a few others are also. He said he would be setting up a new company, but not in competition with us."

"He didn't tell me about it."

"I'm sure it'll be a shadow company. If you take out that much money, the government would take a third up to half of it. He'll have to reinvest it in something within a set period of time."

"Why can't I start now?"

"Your family matters are your private business. Keep them out of this place, or you won't work here. Jack has a right to move his stuff out at his own pace. You can start next week. Is there anything else?"

She was surprised at his gruffness. He had always treated her nicer before. She had a job, and she thought she should quit while she was ahead. Kate just shook her head and left. Now she wondered how friendly a place it would be. Jack had been very successful at making lots of money.

For Jack, the last six days had been the roughest since he lost Sara. The Marriot had been his temporary home until Joe Bivens offered his old house. He could have stayed at the apartment in New York, but Kate wanted it. Glen Cove was getting farther from New York every day. Jack would not be going into the city very often now. Jack moved into the small ten-thousand-square-foot home, only needing his clothes. Jack's good business sense had made Joe a lot of money, and this allowed him to give back to Jack just a little. Like Jack's home, this one had a pool and a great view of the ocean. Jack had full use of the property until he decided what he was going to do. There were two people taking care of the exterior and interior of the home, so he didn't have to worry about the house at all. He spent a lot of time with his son and those other things on his list.

Each morning, Jack would pick up his son and drive him to school. Most seniors drove themselves, but Jere liked the attention from his dad. Jack would then go to the gym and spend a couple of hours. He wasn't in a hurry anymore. Now, around ten, he would sit by the pool and read the paper. He could hear the birds and the surf going about their business. He was sad but at peace.

Victor and Kim had been busy all week packing up Jack's stuff and moving out of the office area that Kate would soon occupy. They were leaving, but anyone else who wanted to stay could. Victor and Kim were setting up shop in the same building but a few floors higher up. Fitzgerald Group owned the space and would be letting Jack use it until he decided what he would be doing.

In total, eight people left their nice, secure jobs to go with Jack. He had 400 million to play with and could afford for his people to do nothing for a while. His legal advisor, Dave, would keep one foot in each camp. He would be busy right now working on Jack's divorce papers. In an unusual move, Kate and Jack were using the same attorney. If Kate wasn't happy with the paperwork, then she could find her own.

Victor and Kim were staying with Jack. Victor had been in Texas when he ran into Jack, but Victor also had family in the New York City area. His daughter was a student at NYCU. Victor's next move would be retirement. Whenever he stopped working for Jack, then he would retire. Kim was single with one daughter still at home. She needed some security, but she trusted Jack. She'd still be coming to the same building, just staying on the elevator for a couple more floors. The Fitzgerald Group had used the office space about ten years earlier. Recently, it had only been used for storage.

Friday,
DECEMBER 8, 2000

On senior night and Jere's last home football game, Jack was the only parent that showed up. He'd had a great year, and some colleges were talking to him about playing defensive end for them. In school, his grades were okay, but not as good as they could have been. Jack was satisfied with the situation. If he had been at home with Jere, he knew Jere's grade point would have been higher.

Jere had a date after the game, so Jack went home. There on the kitchen table lay his divorce papers, still unsigned. Kate had signed them. The judge had approved them. He just needed to sign them. The papers also changed his name to Jack Allen. Jonathon Allen Fitzgerald died with the stroke of a pen.

Kate had wanted what was hers, but not more. Jack was also willing to divide their holdings. The judge was amazed at how civil it was. Basically, Kate wanted to keep their old lifestyle, and Jack was willing to let her keep it. He had told Maggie, Mario, and Tony to stay with Kate because he wasn't sure what he'd be doing.

Jack went to Joe Blevin's bar, intending to make a big martini. Tears rolling down his face, he exchanged the tumbler for a small glass. Jere would be spending the night at his place, so he needed his wits. Jack liked listening to Brickman piano music. It always made him feel better. Tonight he needed the music. He couldn't stop thinking about the night Kate told him to leave. He was no longer crying tears, but he was crying. His whole body ached, and he had trouble walking. He sort of waddled out to look at the surf. The cold sea breeze chilled his large frame, but he could feel.

In a few short weeks, he had lost his daughter, and now tonight, he signed away his Kate. Jere only had five months left, and then he might go off as well. Jack sipped his martini and wondered where all the time had gone. After a bit, he moved in behind the glass doors and fell asleep watching the surf.

I n a bar on Austin's Sixth Street, a couple of grad students were scoping out the place. Marcus and Al were amazed at the number of young people in the bar every night. When Al was an undergrad, he'd averaged four hours of sleep a night. Life was good. Both guys were free and looking to hook up with a beauty tonight.

"Hey, Al. You know you don't have to be here alone tonight. Barb would take you back in a minute."

"Yeah, I know. She just doesn't fit right."

"Man, I don't understand you. She's a great fit."

"Was I in school with you last year?"

"Stupid, you were working on a boat for a year, earning grad money."

"Just before I finished that year, we made a port stop in Cancun. We were there for four days. I met someone I think I would like to spend the rest of my life with."

"You gotta be shittin' me. You've never told me this story before. She was a great lover with tons of money, right?"

"I never slept with her. We visited one time for about half an hour, and then she went off with her friends."

"What, you never saw her again?"

"My last night in port, I saw her and started to go over and talk with her. But this other guy Rick beat me to her. They had a drink together, and then they left together."

"Wow. That love story ended quickly. You never saw her again?"

"Not exactly, he seemed to be helping her walk. I went outside to check on her and was mugged."

"That bitch set you up."

"No, I don't think so. Either I was mugged or I was stopped. I mean they didn't want me following them."

"Your mind is playing games with you, dude. She chose this Rick guy, and then they got married."

"He didn't seem to be the marrying kind. He seemed pretty sleazy. I think there's another Cancun trip in my future."

"You told me that whole story just to justify going to Cancun. You sly devil, you."

Their conversation was interrupted by two blond coeds. "Hey guys, want to split some buffalo wings with us?"

The boys looked at each other and knew they wanted to stay in college forever.

Friday,
DECEMBER 22, 2000

I t was the Christmas season, and Anka knew she was a sparkling ornament for Ibrahim's arm. Life in the casino had never been more active. He had as much business as he wanted, turning down as much as 70 percent of those asking to come. His wasn't entertainment for the family. He didn't want people coming to see pirates. He was looking for real pirates in hopes of making deals with them. In fact, many of his customers were people he had dealings with. Neither trusted the other, and that was the way he liked it.

As Ibrahim's girl, she didn't have to do anything else. Tonight she was watching the two new girls wait on tables, when Rebecca came up from behind her.

"Good evening, Anka."

Anka knew of Rebecca but had never talked with her. At thirty, Rebecca was Ibrahim's oldest daughter. She ran the small school for those living on the island. "Evening, Miss Balta."

"Please. I'm just Rebecca. There is a lot of activity down there tonight."

"There is, every night."

They exchanged niceties for a few minutes, and then Rebecca revealed her reason for her visit. "I know that you are special to my father, his girlfriend. I'm not sure of the right English word. But I want to go to Singapore and buy some things. I asked him if I could take you. At first, he was surprised. He said your visa had expired, but he could get you a new one. Would you like to go with me?"

"Sure." It would be impossible to escape, but just getting off the island would be great.

"Father has made reservations for us at the Plaza in Singapore. I'm so excited to get off this island."

Anka just smiled as Rebecca walked away. She felt lighthearted for the first time in a while. She hadn't noticed it, but she had become melancholy because of the Christmas season. Maybe this was Ibrahim's gift to her. She spotted the two new girls again and wondered how they were doing.

By the twenty-second, Jack got his copy of the signed and approved divorce papers. Jack was single again. He and Jere got off the plane just after noon. There was still a lot of sun left in the day. They checked into the Grand Palace and unpacked. Jack had come to check out the Spirit Club. It was to become his, right after the Christmas break. Jere had come along to see Cancun. This place had swallowed up his sister a few months earlier, and he needed to come and check it out.

"I met the mother of the other missing girl, Veronica. I think I'll give her a call and let her know we're in town."

"Sure, Dad. I'll check out the beach."

The Grand Palace was located next to the tourist center and mall area. There in the mall area was Jack's new business. This two-week period was almost as busy as spring break. Then it would get slow for a few weeks, waiting on spring break to arrive.

Christi was watching her boss to see if he was being watched. Even after he went to his room, she stayed to see if anyone left. One lady closed her magazine and went outside. She made a phone call and then started walking toward the tourist center. Christi followed. There a policeman met up with her, and they talked. He gave her a kiss and slipped something into her pocket. He had just paid to learn that Jack had arrived.

"Hello. Is Laura home?"

"Who's calling, please?"

"Uh, it's Jack Allen."

"You don't sound so sure, Mr. Allen."

"I'm not sure she'll remember my name, but our daughters turned up missing the same night."

"I'm sorry, Mr. Allen, but we get a bunch of bad calls. Mom's not here right now, but I'll have her call you when she gets back. Do you want to give me your number?" Letti's English was perfect, except for her Mexican pronunciation.

"Listen, Letti. Tell her that I'm in town this week with my son, and we wanted to invite the two of you out to dinner. Tell her to call the Grand Palace."

"Mr. Allen, we accept. We can be there at six, okay?"

"If you're sure it's okay with your mother, then we'll see you at six." A smile returned to his face that had been lost for a while. Now to find his son and tell him who was coming to dinner.

Ibrahim chided himself, "You are getting soft in your old age." He had instructed Rebecca to tell Anka that she was to catch the next plane back to Prague. He had seen her put on a good show, but he knew it was only a show. She had been good to him, and he would do something he had never done before. He would release a captive.

Rebecca and Anka took the ferry to the mainland. From there, they flew to Singapore. When they landed, Rebecca gave Anka her ticket to Prague.

Anka knew what the ticket was, but she couldn't believe it. "What's this?"

"It's your freedom. Father wants you to go home."

Anka heard words she had given up on, but she wasn't alone. "What about the other girls?"

"Father is a king in a way. He rules our island the way his father did and his father. When he is gone and Ben is in control, we will release anyone wanting to leave. Until that time, I can do nothing."

Anka hugged Rebecca and walked off to her flight. She felt great and guilty at the same time. In her ticket was an account number with her pass code. Ibrahim had given her money as well. Ten hours of flying seemed like an eternity, but then she landed in Prague.

Robert Casper went to the door, wondering who would be out at ten. He might be at a bar, but not going visiting. He opened the door to Anka. She was six years older, but his Anka was home.

"Beata, come here!" He was crying with joy.

Beata was wondering why Robert was screaming at her. She could have heard him in a normal voice. She had just settled into bed and was going to read a little before she slept. "Robert, you don't have to yell." As her eyes fell on the open door, she couldn't speak. Her hands went to her mouth, and she started crying. Her Anka had come back. She couldn't even think about where she might have been.

Anka moved over to her mother and held her. Anka cried also. Parents and daughter thought this day would never come. The three of them had cried for each other so many nights, and now they were together. "Mama, I'm so sorry for the way I've acted in the past. I'm so sorry." They just held each other.

Then a surprised Robert received a command from his wife. "Get the Becherovka, some salt, and some bread. She has to be greeted the right way." It was the formal greeting for a weary traveler.

Surprised and smiling, Anka said, "Mama, you don't have to do that."

"Robert, don't make me tell you again."

Anka cried and laughed as she took the bread and dipped it in the salt. Then they all toasted and drank their Becherovka. It was strong, so they each had a little water as well. Robert and Beata would not be going to work for a few days.

Johnny had Christi watching Jack. The bad people might be checking him out. Her watching had paid off. Someone wanted to know more about Jack. Lieutenant Diaz wanted to know more about this gringo, but there was nothing. Jack Allen was not his real name, and Captain Sanchez would not release his fingerprints so he could search further. Why would Jack Allen pay top price for the Spirit Club?

Christi had followed the man back to the police station, where he met up with a police lieutenant. The lieutenant smiled and went back inside. Jack had notified the captain that he was coming, so this man was not working with the captain. It must have been Lieutenant Noe Diaz. She would talk to Johnny about whether to tell Jack.

When Letti told Laura they were meeting Jack at six, she was not able to say anything. She just smiled. Her heart had done one of those young-love things, but it was okay now. She just hoped her daughter hadn't noticed.

"Hey, Mom. I noticed."

"What did you notice?"

"I saw you gasp and hold your heart when I said *Jack!*"

"Stop it. I can go alone, you know."

"Parents can be so mean."

When they walked up to the Grand Palace, both were acting like two nervous teenage girls. Letti saw their reflection in the mirrored hotel window and showed her mother. "Mom, we must be confident!" They laughed and walked in.

There in the lobby were their two men, acting like two nervous teenage boys meeting up with their dates. Laura and Letti looked at each other and laughed.

"Jack, this is my daughter Letti. She's a senior this year."

"And this is my son, Jere. He's a senior this year. Wait. Did I already say that?"

Now Laura reached up and kissed Jack on the cheek. Letti kissed him next, and they both kissed Jere. The two young people talked together, and that freed Laura and Jack to talk openly.

"How are things back in New York?"

"Things have really changed. Kate divorced me. She has the house. I'm living in a friend's house until I move down here."

"Move here? Why?"

"Lots of reasons. I hired a detective to see what he could find out. He found out that the owner was getting ready to sell the Spirit Club, so I bought it. I wanted to keep it the same, just in case someone or some clue returned. I plan on searching for Sara for a couple of years. After that, if I've found nothing, then I'll go forward as if she's not coming back. I have plenty of time and money, so why not see if I can find out what happened? Sara's my daughter, and I'm willing to use my assets to find her. Soon Jere will be out of school. I hope he goes to college next year, but he hasn't decided what he wants to do yet. Basically, I'm free to look for her."

"Jack, you can't stay here. You have a business to run. All those people are counting on you."

"No. I sold my shares. My friend, Frank, is running the company, and I'm free to do what I want for a change."

Letti saw them touching with their eyes even though they weren't holding hands, so she grabbed Jere's hand and pulled him farther down the beach. They walked and talked and enjoyed the evening.

When they came back, Jack offered the ladies a ride home.

"Can we drop you off?"

"No, thank you, Jack. Number17 will get us home."

One more kiss and brush of the cheek. One more whiff of perfume. "Call us when you are free tomorrow."

"*Bueno*, bye."

For Christmas, the Fitzgerald estate was prettier than it had ever been, but there was a gray cloud hanging over it. A year before, a happy family had lived there. Now just a wealthy woman and her son stayed there. Jere had agreed to stay until after graduation, and then he would be leaving too. Kate would have the estate all to herself.

Kate had gone to the Christmas party, but it wasn't much fun. She had prestige, but it only lasted until about eight. Like an alarm clock, Sara had popped into Kate's mind. Sara would have celebrated her nineteenth birthday tomorrow. But now she wouldn't have any more. That was when it was time for Kate to head home. The party spirit had left her.

Now sitting on her sofa in her beautiful, quiet home, she second-guessed herself one more time. And one more time, she poured one more drink. Tonight was another night on the sofa. If she moved, she might fall down. She might wake up and not be able to sleep. So one more night spent on the sofa. She thought to herself, *Merry Christmas, Jack and Jere.*

The doorbell surprised her. No one should have been able to get through the gate. When she opened the door, she was surprised again—she was looking at Brad Caster. "Yes, Brad. How can I help you? Are you lost?" Her speech was a bit slurred.

Brad had been planning to make a move on her tonight, but she had left early. Now his nerves were weakening. "I . . . uh . . . saw you leave early, and I wanted to make sure you were okay."

In her condition, when she turned to move, she tripped. Brad was quick and caught her. On impulse, he kissed her. Nothing happened, so he stopped. He then saw that she was very drunk and kissed her again.

This time, Kate responded. In Kate's clouded, drunken state, she was kissing Jack.

Still kissing her, he picked her up and carried her to the couch. He had to help her get out of her clothes. Her silk blouse came off easily, but he fumbled with her bra. She was prettier than he had hoped. Next came her skirt and slip. While they disrobed, they continued to kiss. Kate helped him with her panties.

Kate was aroused by her Jack. His hands moved differently, but that was okay. He was giving her long-needed affection and attention.

Brad was very excited now as he almost tore off his clothes. They made love once for Brad and then again for Kate. Exhausted and drunk, Kate passed out. Brad was too tired to move. Tonight was way more than he had hoped for. After a little rest, he got up and carried her to bed. There he cleaned her a little and put her into some PJs. Then he lay down next to her and slept.

A couple of hours later, they made love again. Her mind still cloudy, she thought Jack had come back to her. But as the sun rose and Kate stirred, she remembered nothing after leaving the party. She was very hungover. Her vision was blurred, and she wasn't sure who was in bed with her. "What are you doing here?"

Brad needed to check out how much she remembered from the night before. "Are you telling me you don't remember anything about last night?" He had counted on her not remembering much. He had had a great time.

"Nooo." Her *no* was more like a moan.

"I'll fix you something."

"No. Nothing."

"I meant medicine." Brian was not looking for love. He was looking for sex. He hoped this was the beginning of an affair where she would pay for everything and he would help her forget about her family.

Ronnie and Sara had made it through the Christmas party the evening before, but barely. Now they were in the apartment they shared. They had held each other all night. Sara said a silent prayer for her family, hoping they were okay, knowing they would miss her. This was her first Christmas away from home.

This morning, Sara woke up determined not to be the victim any longer. "Ronnie, let's go and get some breakfast."

Ronnie was not a morning person. "No. Go away."

"Okay. But I may not be back all day." Yosef had given the girls the day off. They were free to go anywhere on the island. She knew that Ronnie had wanted to go walking. When the guards weren't watching, they were sure cameras were. They just wanted to be out and away from being watched.

"I'll remember this, lady."

Soon they were off. "I didn't tell you, but I'm nineteen today. And I've decided to stop being the victim. I didn't do anything to get here. I think I'll try tending bar."

Ronnie didn't know the girl she was walking with. "Where is Sara, and what have you done to her?"

"You've been telling me all along that I've done nothing to deserve this. Well, I believe you. Now I'm going to have some fun until I can figure out how to get out of here. I've always wanted to tend bar."

"You're serious, aren't you?"

"Duh, yes."

Laura and Jack had enjoyed talking about their daughters and getting to know each other. Jere and Letti had a great time. Today Letti talked Jere into checking out the after-Christmas sale at Walmart. They spent very little time with the old people.

That evening, the young people visited a disco, and Jack and Laura returned to the Spirit Club. After two of the mystery drinks, Jack was willing to make a fool of himself, and so he danced. At first, he danced so she would stop nagging him. Then he danced because he liked it. Then he danced to be next to her. Jack wasn't sure he was supposed to like dancing with Laura so soon after his divorce.

"I think I need to go back to the hotel. I'm not used to this."

"Si, senior."

But her heart was saying other things. This gringo stirred her blood. She couldn't talk seriously with him now. Her hope was that her daughter wouldn't say too much. Letti seemed to see some things before she did.

When they left, they were holding hands, and Jack liked it. He was not ready for any kind of relationship, but he liked being around Laura. Back at the hotel, he asked again if he could take them home.

"Bus 17 will do. Thank you." She reached up to kiss him on the cheek but caught a little of his lip. He tasted good. She shivered as the thought raced through her.

He held her and told her, "Thanks for another wonderful Cancun night."

Neither wanted to let go. This seemed to be a really good fit. Then he let her go and walked to the elevator. Jere tagged along behind.

As Jack laid his head on his pillow, a tear came to his eye. Today Sara turned nineteen. This was the first time they had not been together at Christmas. His body ached as he wondered where she was and how she was doing. Then he drifted off to sleep.

The next morning, Jere and Letti were getting together, but Jack had some business to take care of. Victor brought Dave Hudson to Cancun to meet Jack. Victor had decided that Dave was the right person to run the club, but Jack would need to approve. Introductions were made, and then Victor told Dave the truth.

"Dave, I haven't told you the whole truth. I don't own the company. Jack does. We don't want you to be the executive assistant. We want you to run the club. Jack is Jonathon Fitzgerald. He used to own the Fitzgerald Group. Then his daughter turned up missing here in Cancun. The last place she was seen was right here. Jack wants you to run the club, and he'll simply be here to sign everything you give him. I'll come down from time to time to inspect, but you'll be running the club. Jack wants to check on any clues or leads that might turn up."

"And when Jack is satisfied with his search, then what do I do for a living?"

"It will still be my club, and you will be my manager."

They agreed on everything. Dave agreed to stay a couple of days to evaluate the current staff.

"Victor, I need you to take Jere back to New York with you. I'll stay a few more days and work with Dave and see where I'm going to live down here."

Jere was not ready to go back to New York, but he knew he would be going back.

Tony was there to pick up Jere at JFK. Kate was at another function, so Jere went home to the big empty estate. For Jere, home had stopped being home the night his father left. It had become like a hotel where he was just a guest. Before, when his father was gone, his mother was always around. Now she was always gone, and his dad lived in another home. The kidnappers had also stolen his home.

Jack busied himself with stuff that seemed important but wasn't. He was trying not to think about Laura Sanchez. But he couldn't get her out of his mind. Kate was there, but was Laura also allowed there? He was divorced from Kate. He was divorced from Kate because she still wanted to live a lifestyle that no longer fit him. Still, he wouldn't let himself phone the person that set him at ease and made him smile. Laura would have to wait. Would she wait?

Sunday,
DECEMBER 31, 2000

Jack came home to Glen Cove for the New Year's Eve celebration. He had wanted to stay longer, but this was Jere's school break. Jack had him for only a short time. Jere was at a party but would be staying the night with Jack. For Jack, it was another quiet night at home. He walked along the beach, listening to the surf and thinking about Cancun and a couple of girls that didn't come home one night.

For Kate, the power and prestige held up until midnight. People were kissing everyone. She had more to drink than she should have, so Brad took the chance. He kissed her more than the usual peck. "You need me to drive you home. You've had too much to drink."

"I'll be all right. Go away."

"Come on. You know I'm right." He led her to the door, and they kept walking. He was surprised. The drive to the estate lasted just thirty minutes, but Kate was pretty much asleep. He helped her inside and to her bedroom. She tried to say something, but her mouth wouldn't work right. Brad became more sexually aroused with each passing moment. Kate had given in to the alcohol and was in a sort of stupor. Hurriedly, Brad removed her clothes. He couldn't get them off quickly enough. He was winded by the time he got to her undergarments. She was too drunk to help with her underwear items. In a sick kind of way, he was glad that Kate wasn't helping him undress her.

When he finished, he paused only for a moment before removing his clothes. Brian was breathing very hard now. He had to rest for a moment, so he just lay next to her. She was beautiful, and tonight she was his. He reached over and woke her as he kissed her. She resisted a moment and then kissed him back. As drunk as she was, she still responded to his lovemaking. For more than an hour, they kissed, bit, clung, and copulated. As drunk as she was, she thought it was Jack and knew that it wasn't in the same moment. It doesn't take much to trick a mind that wants to be fooled. And then Brad and Kate slept.

Kate woke up not remembering the night before. She knew she had sex, but she didn't remember anything. She was still groggy as she made her way to the bathroom. There in her bed lay Brad, again.

Kate needed affection. She was getting some, but it was only lust. She couldn't remember the end of the party or any of the sex. She looked into the mirror and wondered who she was looking at. Her neck showed signs of her play from the night before. Her eyes showed signs of her drinking. Kate decided this would not be her future lifestyle. The drinking would have to be limited to just one glass. If she were to have any boyfriends, it would be down the road and not right now.

It was time for the sleeping beast to wake up. "Brad, wake up and go home. We're not doing this anymore. You work for the company, and so it's over."

Brad was surprised but wasn't willing to give up. "Kate, maybe we could do lunch or something."

"No. You've been here twice when I've had too much to drink. That stops now, so you won't be coming here ever again!"

During the next few weeks, Kate started trying to give Jere more attention. But he was still too angry with her. Work was just the opposite. Frank gave her some easy projects she did really well on, so he gave her more and more. Soon she wasn't Jack's ex. She was Kate Fitzgerald.

Her time was totally hers. Like going to work every day at FGNY, she began working out every day. The intensified workouts made her look and feel great. Her social calendar was always full. But night would come, and Jack wasn't there. In the darkness before she fell asleep, there was always time to think about Sara. Motherly feelings never go away. She would remember a little girl playing with Christmas toys and the boxes they came in. While washing dishes one day, she saw Jack pulling Sara around in the snow in the front yard in her good clothes basket. They were both laughing and having a great time. Another time, Jack had raked a big pile of leaves, and she watched Jack, Sara, and Jere rolling around in them—priceless memories.

Now she regretted pushing Jack away. He had been devastated by the loss of his little girl. At night, in the darkness, there was nowhere to go. Kate would cry. When she was honest with herself, she knew she loved that man. Soon he would be in Mexico. Jere was so grown-up and looked so much like a young Jack. Still with tears in her eyes, she drifted off to sleep. The tears tonight were happy tears, satisfied tears.

Saturday,

FEBRUARY 3, 2001

R onnie was the first one to mention her name. "I miss Anka."
"We shouldn't talk about her. I'm sure they are listening to us."
"Okay."

Ronnie was a dealer, and Sara was tending bar. They didn't mind working because it kept their minds busy. Neither had figured out how to get off the island, but they were still trying to come up with some plan. Except for the fact that they were captives, the girls lived and dressed well. Their clothes were of Asian design, and most were made from silk and other expensive cloth. Ronnie thought she might have chosen to work there if she had been given a choice. The fact was, they were captives, all nineteen of them.

Saad knocked on the door.

Sara answered, "We are almost ready, Saad."

Saad looked like the French inspector from the old movies, but he was from Iraq. He had left Iraq and headed toward America to seek his fortune. He just seemed to have gotten sidetracked. For the last ten years, he had been working for Ibrahim. "Mr. Ibrahim has said that you are not working tonight. You are to come with me."

Both were very nervous. They had just been talking about Anka, and then Saad showed up.

He sensed their apprehension. "Don't worry, ladies. This is good news. Come."

They walked along a cobblestone road, toward where the Baltas lived. Then Saad took them down a walkway to a new condo. It was facing the ocean, and the view was amazing.

"Mr. Ibrahim said this is your new home. You have made him much money, and he is very happy. Please keep him happy." The home was beautiful, but they were still captives.

Ibrahim was having some Turkish tea alone. He'd rather be alone than with someone who bothered him. He missed his Anka. She had been his best female friend, but he had to get rid of her. She would have found out about his prostate cancer. It was a slow-growing cancer. So if he had no treatments, he could live five or six years. He hadn't told his family and wasn't going to. His doctor was a pirate like him and would tell no one. He could hide it from his managers and family, but he wouldn't have been able to keep it from Anka. She would be his last girlfriend. It was time to make his set of twenty complete again. He would send Maged back to find one more beauty for his collection. He would send him far away, where it would be safe to snatch an unsuspecting lady.

"Ronnie. What are we going to do? I love this place, but we are prisoners."

"I know, Sara. Let's go for a walk."

Both knew that the walls would have ears. Outside in the breeze, they wouldn't be heard. They were living on a tropical island. Now they had a beautiful view of the sea. They could see other islands far off, but they had no idea where they were.

To their amazement, they hadn't been used as whores. They were like dolls that people could only look at but not touch. The last girl touched had been Anka, by Ibrahim, and now she was gone. He had killed two other girls, and now Anka was gone. She must have done something wrong or tried to escape. "We can't let Ibrahim choose one of us, or we might go away like Anka went away."

"Sara, she might have made it out."

"Neither of us believes that."

"I know. We'll have to be careful."

Johnny Trudle and Christi Douglas had been working on the kidnapping nonstop all these months. Finally, using some mathematical deductions, they were making headway. Eighteen months earlier, Johnny and Christi had been cops in Jersey City. Johnny had finally gotten his fill of the police jumping through hoops while the bad guys set them on fire. Johnny didn't hop one time when his captain told him to, and that was the end for Johnny. He got his man but left the police force. Now he was going to follow his rules and not those that civilian cops must follow. It wasn't long until Christi followed him out the door. Together they formed a detective agency, Finders. Finding Sara had been their first big case. Johnny came by the Spirit Club from time to time, but he never met with Jack there. They met at an old hotel, not far from the beach, and on the mainland.

Johnny began, "Be patient with me as I go over what we have. We haven't heard from the girls, nor do we have their bodies. If they are dead, then they are buried. I don't think this is the case. From the photos and histories you've given me, I've determined that both girls were taken because they were simply beautiful. There have been no ransom notes or messages of any kind. I think Sara and Veronica were kidnapped to be used as white slaves.

"If that's the case, and I think it is, we need to get them away from Cancun. Trains and air travel are out. They would go kicking and screaming, or you would need to drug them. Can't get them on a train or plane that way, but you can a ship. Lock them in a room, and they can kick and scream all they want.

"You can't put teens kicking and screaming or drugged on a tourist liner. The boat would need to be a cargo ship or a tanker. It's probably not registered in the Americas. I've contacted the port authority here."

Jack was tired of what was not. He wanted to know what was. "Cut to the chase, Johnny. Do you have a ship identified?"

"We do. It's a tanker, the *Verdi Mare*. It seems to be owned by the Eastern Green Sea Shipping Corporation out of Singapore. It's somehow connected to a corporation named Basic Arabic Limited Trading Alliance. The ship's captain is a naturalized US citizen whose family is living in Florida. He's a former Egyptian. The tanker is in port on a small island named Balta. It's not far from Jakarta. The owner of the company is Adnan Kareem. I'm guessing that the girls were taken to the island of Balta and then maybe on to their final destination."

Jack was impressed. "Good. Keep working on it."

Wednesday,
MARCH 28, 2001

Yosef Daniel and Ibrahim had gone over the books and were now enjoying a drink together. Yosef was his closest friend. "Tell me what you hear around the island."

"It is said that Ibrahim is sick and dying. It is said that you sent Anka away or she escaped, which is worse. Adnan has spies watching us."

"And I have spies watching him. Adnan will get his just rewards. I don't believe in god, so I will provide him his punishment when the time is right."

"What about Anka?"

"Let it slip that she tried to escape on a shopping trip and was eliminated."

"What about being sick?" Yosef looked at his boss, hoping there would be a quick denial. When none came, he offered a solution. "You need to choose a new girl."

"I am already working on that."

Friday,
MAY 4, 2001

B y March, Jack was living full-time in Mexico. The Grand Palace had given him a special deal on a large suite on the second floor. He had come back to New York for Jere's graduation ceremony in May, and then he and Jere returned to Cancun. In the six months that Jack had had the Spirit Club, he hadn't changed much at the club, just some paint here and there. Dave was running the club with the title of executive assistant. Jack was watching and learning the club business. The old manager had left, but much of the old staff stayed. Dave would coach Jack on what to say in front of the staff, so no one knew that Jack was faking it. No one was really allowed to approach Jack with questions. Everything went through Dave.

Jack's one suggestion for hiring had been to employ Laura Santos. She was local and, of course, understood the language. Both Dave and Jack were learning Spanish, so one of the assistants had to do most of the translating. Often it was Laura.

Saad showed up at the condo in the afternoon to speak with Veronica. "Tonight you will have a date with Ibrahim. You should hold on to his arm and walk with him wherever he goes. Speak when spoken to. Since this will be your first time out with him, I suggest you just watch. Don't ask his guests any questions. Much of their business is not legal, and you don't really want to know what they do. He wants his guests to see him with one of his beautiful dolls. He will give you instructions as far as what you should eat or drink around him. He is not a difficult man to please. Just do as he says."

"Do I have a choice?"

"Of course not!"

"What should I wear?"

"Just come to the casino at five. You will be taken to a room to prepare. They will have all you need there."

"Okay, Saad." The *okay* didn't convey the fear that she felt. She would be next to her captor. She would be with other pirates as well.

"Do not be afraid of Ibrahim. You are not as much for him as you are for his guests to see him with you. He is a tired old man who must keep up a certain image. You will be part of that image. Also, you will be sleeping at the casino tonight, but not with Ibrahim."

At five, Ronnie arrived at the casino and was escorted to a spa. There she was given the full royal treatment. Every inch of her body was rubbed, oiled, and cleaned. Her hair was washed, cut, set, and styled. Her nails were painted and polished. Her clothes fit like they had been made for her, and they had. When she came out three hours later, she looked ready for her celebrity photo shoot. She was, without a doubt, the prettiest woman on the island, and it had only taken three hours.

Saad came for her and led her to Ibrahim. "Sir, Veronica." He bowed and stepped aside.

Ibrahim was looking at the prettiest young lady he had ever laid eyes on. She was tall, with glistening black hair. Her lips were dark red, and her large dark eyes were lined to make them even larger and more impressive. He was very pleased with himself. Again he had selected a beauty.

"When I want you to come with me, I will tell you. We will all sit and eat supper together. You will be the only female in the room. Later the others will be joined by female companions, but not for supper. The guests are my business associates and nothing more. Many I don't like, but they make a lot of money for me and allow me to live like I do. Tonight you will play the role of queen. You will eat with us and then there will be some entertainment and then you will sleep in your private chamber."

With the instructions over, they entered a fabulous dining hall. Instantly, all eyes were on Veronica. Oohs and aahs were heard all over the chamber. Then Ibrahim held up a hand for silence. "My friends, I greet you in peace. Peace unto all. Please enjoy your meal."

Ibrahim sat at the head with his queen sitting next to him. "Gentlemen, this is Veronica." Most of the conversation was in Arabic. From time to time, some English was spoken for her and to her.

Her meal was lobster, with a salad, a baked potato, and some other veggies; but she could only eat a little. She was very nervous and not sure what was happening. What was happening right now was okay, but what was to come?

After the meal was finished, Ali Al Mutari came and asked that everyone follow him. This was not the first time the guests had come to the little private room. No one was surprised by Ali's request. They all went into a small theater room with small couches. Each couch had a girl waiting for the guests. Ibrahim and Ronnie sat off to the side. He motioned for her to sit next to him. This was the time she was afraid of. "Relax, Veronica, you are not the entertainment. It is in front of us."

With a signal to Ali, the curtain opened to reveal two ladies undressing each other. These two were not part of the set of dolls, but they were keeping the attention of the guests. In the little private room, clothes were coming off. In the theater, the same thing was happening. Soon no one was looking at Ibrahim and Ronnie. "This may be disgusting to you, but it is not for you. It is for them and their little brains. For me, this is only a business matter." Ibrahim stood up, and Ronnie left with him. No one seemed to notice they had left.

Next Saad met them outside the chamber and took Ronnie to her suite for the night. "Is that it?"

"Yes, you are finished for the night."

"But I'm not leaving the casino?"

"Yes. You are staying the night in this suite. You can have anything brought to you that you want."

"Can I have Sara brought?"

"No. Tonight everyone must think that you spent the night with Ibrahim and that his grieving for Anka is over. It is time to move on."

"Am I his girl now?"

"No. He will choose between you and two others. That's enough questions for tonight."

Now Ronnie needed Sara. She was tired of being the strong one. She wanted Sara to hold her and help her through the night. Ronnie slept off and on during the long night.

Saturday,
MAY 5, 2001

With morning came Saad. She looked the way she felt. "Now we can go home." Saad took her by her wrist and led her out of the suite. "You cannot speak of what went on here last night. If you do, bad things will happen."

"How can I not speak of what went on here? Look at me. I'm a mess."

"If you do, then we will separate you two. Am I clear?"

"Yes."

Ronnie ran into the condo. Going straight to Sara, she jumped into her bed.

"Ronnie, what happened to you?" Sara tried to wipe her face, but Ronnie just cried.

"I can't tell you anything. If I do, they'll separate us. Do you understand? You can't ask me. Just hold me, and I'll be okay." Ronnie wept for an hour. She was a prisoner on an island somewhere in the Orient. All the tears she did not cry were now coming out. Acting strong was over. Now she just wanted Sara to hold her. Sara held her, and they both slept.

Ronnie wouldn't let Sara leave for two days. On the third day, they were both ready for a walk in the hills. The weather was beautiful, and the view was amazing as they looked down at all the little boats and people. "What happened was that I remembered we were not free. All of the beauty and wealth all around doesn't mean anything when you are a slave. It really hit home that we have to do what we are told, or else we might die. I missed my mom and family. I missed Cancun."

"How are you doing today?"

"I still miss all of that, but I'm better today. I'll go back to work tomorrow. But this will never be home. Never!"

Ibrahim winded up choosing Diana as his escort. Saad didn't elaborate, but Ibrahim liked Veronica too much and didn't want her around him. He was not looking for a friend. He was only looking for an escort.

Friday,
AUGUST 24, 2001

"Jack, we've been tracking a ship, the *Verdi Mare*, for several weeks. Coming here was not part of its normal route. It did pick up some oil, but you wonder why it never returned. The company that owns it is a private corporation, the Eastern Green Sea Shipping Corporation out of Singapore. It used to be part of the Basic Arabic Limited Traders Alliance, BALTA. I've already briefed you on this, but we've come to a dead end.

"Jack, I'm going over to get closer to the ship and its port to see what I can find out. I don't know how long I'll be gone, but I'll keep in touch."

"Be safe. And thanks." Jack was pleased with the report, but he was halfway through the allotted timetable he'd set. He had given himself twenty-four months, and then he would move on with his life.

Tuesday,
SEPTEMBER 11, 2001

Frank called Kate into his office. She was a friend and coworker now. Bill had called and said he needed to turn on his TV. A plane had just slammed into the World Trade Center. Together they watched the unbelievable. There was a second plane, and then seven buildings were destroyed. From their windows, they could see the smoke. They could see the towers fall. Someone had declared war on America.

Frank didn't panic. He called his staff in and told them to go home and stay with their families for a week. "We're not buying or selling at this time. We will not profit from someone else's misfortune. Go home. Hug your spouse and kids. We'll get together in a week."

The stock exchange closed for a time. For weeks, a city cried and tried to recover her loss. Then when there was no more hope of finding survivors, they looked for closure. Months passed as they removed more and more rubble. It would be six months before they reached the subway levels, and then closure could begin.

That first night, Kate used the apartment in town. Just blocks away, part of her city was burning. Smoke and dust rose into a gray sky. It was as if a dust storm had hit the city as well. Except for the sirens, the city was quiet. Traffic wasn't moving. It was inching forward. Kate walked slowly to her apartment. You would be sad if a few were killed. She knew the number would be in the thousands. Kate was devastated by her city's loss. At the apartment, she just watched the events unfold on her TV. Her cell couldn't get service and her landline phone wasn't working, so she watched and cried.

For most Americans, September 11 was a time of reevaluating your life. Alfred Rendon knew he should have gone to the police and reported what had happened to him. His gut feeling was that something was not right with Sara. Now he knew he would go back to Cancun. His life could not go on until he went back. He didn't know what he would find, but he had to go back and visit the same places and see what might happen.

Sara and Ronnie didn't know about the towers falling. They just knew that they'd been on the island for twelve months. The condo had made life better, but they both knew they were still prisoners.

Wednesday,
SEPTEMBER 12, 2001

S he had slept in Jack's chair. She missed him now more than words could describe. Kate always felt safe and secure in his arms. She had used his coat for a blanket. Jack wasn't there, but his scent was. That helped. Her hand tried to resist orders from her brain to turn the set off, but it did. She showered, but she couldn't wash off the gray feeling she carried deep in her soul, knowing thousands in New York had just died. She left her apartment and began making her way toward Madison Square Garden. Once there, she caught a train up to Glen Cove. From the station in Glen Cove, she just took a taxi home.

Maggie saw her first. "Ms. Kate, are you okay?"

"Yes and no. I can't believe it happened. But I was safe. All of the phones were either busy or out of service."

"Jere called here. He was worried about you, ma'am." Maggie was hopeful for Kate. She knew that she and Jere hadn't had the same relationship they had before Jack left. Her stupid divorce had torn the family apart. She had lost. She had lost Jack, Jere, and Sara.

"Thank you, Maggie." Soon all the help had gathered around her. Tony wanted to know how she had gotten home, and Mario was trying to hug her. For a change, it felt like a home.

"Listen, I'm really okay. I just need to talk to Jere."

"Yes, ma'am. You just tell us if you need anything."

Kate called Jere's cell number and smiled, a little bit nervous. She hadn't spoken to him much since the night she sent Jack away. She had tried, but he never responded. Now he wanted to talk to her.

Jere knew it was her because of his caller ID. "Mom! Are you okay?"

"Yes, son. It's good to hear your voice. How are you doing?"

"I'm fine. Me and Dad were worried about you. We couldn't get through. Mom, you've got to come down here. I mean, as soon as the planes are flying again. I need you. I mean, I need to show you around. This place is great!" Jere had spoken what he felt, but he wasn't sure how his mother would take it. It had been months since he had really had a conversation with her.

"Tell your father that I'll be down in a few days. I love you. Bye." How long had it been since she had said those words to her son, now her only child? It had been more than twelve months since Sara had not returned. Jere had sounded just like his father. She wondered how Jack was.

She thought a moment. Sara had been gone a year now. She wondered if there was really anything she could have done differently. She shook her head. Jere needed her again, so she would go and see her son. She knew she needed Jack, but she didn't know how it would go down in Cancun.

Ben Balta ran the casino for his father, but he didn't know about the smuggling and the weapons being sold through their shipping business. Adnan Kareem was in charge of the shipping business and was a true pirate. His father had worked for Ibrahim's father, and now for forty years, he had been doing Ibrahim's bidding. The casino only made a very small profit compared to the profits Adnan had realized the last ten years. If he thought he could get away with it, he would kill anyone and take anything he wanted. Lately he had been looking at the Mexican beauty. He had tried to talk Ibrahim into giving her to him. Ibrahim wouldn't hear of it. The twenty ladies were like his collector's toys. He was not willing to share them with anyone. Adnan thought that one day that would change, but he wasn't ready to challenge Ibrahim just yet.

What he could do would be to have Rick find two more ladies in Cancun. Ibrahim would be expecting one, and he would give him one. The other one he would keep for himself. Ibrahim knew that Adnan could not be trusted. So one of his top aides would be a spy for Ibrahim. He didn't know which one, so he would only share the details of his plan with Rick.

Ibrahim called Saad in for his daily morning briefing. "*Salem*, my friend." Ibrahim greeted his friend with the normal three kisses. They weren't really kisses. Cheeks were brushed and a sound of kissing made.

"*Salem.*"

"Tell me what's happening on my island."

"There is a new face on Bird Island. He is not a relative of anyone. We think he is from New York. Your newest girl, Sara, is from New York. He does not mention her name, but he has been asking a lot of questions about your island."

"Good, Saad. Keep an eye on him." Then they discussed the other business of the island.

Kate was staying at the Hilton on the beach. She hadn't bothered to call Jere yet. She wanted to see Jack, so she stopped by the Spirit Club. She was wearing shorts and a halter top that looked cool, but she wasn't. Her nerves were weakening. The first person she saw was Laura. "Excuse me. Is Jack in?"

Laura knew Kate from the photos she had looked at with Jack, but she played dumb. "We're not really open yet. Do you have an appointment with Mr. Allen?"

"I think he'll see his ex-wife. Are you his current?" Her claws were out.

Laura was having a good time with Kate. She didn't answer her question. She spun and said, "Follow me, please." Laura used her sexiest walk as she led Kate back to Jack's office. She walked in and kissed him on the cheek, leaving red lipstick on purpose. "Ms. Fitzgerald to see you."

To Laura, he said, "We're being bad, aren't we?" Her eyes said yes.

"Come in, Kate, and have a seat. Would you like anything?"

To Laura, Kate said, "Could you leave us alone, please?"

Jack watched Laura wiggle on out, and Kate watched Jack watch Laura.

"Kate, you look great!"

"You look good too, Jack."

In the next room, Laura was wondering how Kate could have divorced Jack. Then she went about getting the Spirit Club ready for opening.

Jack was still smiling at Laura. She had wanted to make Kate know she had let him go.

In the brief silence, Kate really looked at Jack. He had speckles of gray in his hair. She couldn't remember him having them before. He was very tanned and toned. The stress was gone from his face. He seemed so relaxed, so handsome. She hadn't seen him in several months. She had avoided him at graduation. Now she was looking at the man she dreamed of at night. "Cancun looks to be good for you."

"Thanks, Kate. New York is pretty bad, huh?"

"Frank and I watched the Towers fall. It was like it wasn't really happening. Then dust or dirt or something filled the air. We all just had to leave. I spent the first night at the apartment in the big recliner and then took the train home the next day. Tell me what you've found out about our daughter."

"There's been no body. We believe Sara and Ronnie, Laura's daughter, were kidnapped. We have no proof, just ideas." Jack didn't want to tell her specifics.

"That's all? Jack, there's more. You're just not telling me."

"You're right. I'm just not telling you more."

Kate was a little more than upset. She was ready to lash out at Jack. "Jack, I'm trying to stay calm. I'm not some reporter. I'm Sara's mother, damn it."

"Everything you've said is correct, but I'm not saying anything else. You are in New York. If anything slipped out, it could cost Sara her life. We are only following up on some ideas, checking things out. It's like no bodies, so maybe something else happened. When it dead-ends, then we'll go a different way. That's all. You just have to trust me."

"I don't agree with you, but I'll let it go for now. Where's my son?"

"Let's go find him. He's with Monica. You'll like her."

Kate spent the whole day with them. By late afternoon, Kate was wearing down. They had a wonderful day. Cancun was showing off for them with her calm breezes, blue water, busy market, and great food. After their Texas steaks, Kate was ready to call it a day. "You two have worn me out. I need to sleep for two days now."

Jere hadn't known whether or not he'd lost his mother in New York a few days earlier. He was hoping she would stay a couple of days. "Mom, you're not going back tomorrow, are you?"

"No, son, I came down for a couple of days." She was planning to stay exactly two days.

"Good then, now we can go by the Spirit Club and see it in action. You'll love it, Mom."

Kate was tired, but this would give her a chance to see Jack again. "I guess so. But just for a few minutes. I'm really tired." Afternoon had quickly moved into evening.

It was a Friday night in Cancun. The Spirit Club had live music playing and tons of people. Kate was impressed. Jere took them to a table with a Reserved sign on it. He told his mom, "We keep this table open for special guests. Tonight that's you."

Kate noticed Laura standing next to Jack before they were spotted.

When Jack saw them, he immediately went over. "May I join you for a bit?"

Kate answered, because Jere and Monica had taken off to dance. "Sure."

Jack ordered two King Spirits. It was a fruit juice with a kick. He watched Kate admiring her son. Jack did it too.

"He's grown a little more. He's tanned, of course, but he seems stronger, healthier."

"I have him busing tables. It's physical work, and he can still interact with any customer of his choosing."

Jere and Monica came off the floor and sat down. In that moment, she lost sight of Jack. A little panic struck, and then a voice from behind asked, "Shall we dance?"

"No, Jack. I can't do that stuff."

"You're probably right. Monica, how long would it take you to teach Kate the Latin steps?"

"Only two minutes, Mr. Jack. She'll be great."

"All right, Kate, you've got two minutes. I'll be right back."

Jere and Monica got Kate up, and she was starting to feel the beat. The King Spirit was starting to kick in as well. When Jack returned, she told him, "You get one dance, buddy."

Together they bumped and wiggled to the music. They were laughing and joking. It had been like that first time Jack watched people trying to escape on the dance floor. Kate and Jack drifted back to an earlier time in their lives when they used to go out and have fun. And then the music stopped. They stood there looking at each other, not moving. Then a slow, romantic guitar started playing. Jack held out his hand, and they danced.

She placed her head on the chest of the man she dreamed about. For her, she was home. It had been a long time, but she was home. She pressed herself up against her man and held on. Her knees were weak, and her heart was pounding.

Jack liked how it felt. His mind drifted to sex and love. He needed both. Kate belonged in his arms. She had wanted her freedom to live like she wanted. But he needed her. She was more than just the mother of his children. She was his lifelong love. And now he held her, and she wanted him to hold her. For Kate, she was the happiest she had been all year.

Too soon, the music stopped. Then it started with its fast pace and strong drum rhythms. Kate and Jack were off to the side now and just looking into each other's eyes.

Kate spoke first. "Now what happens?"

"We sit." They just sat where they were. What he wanted to do was hold her and kiss her as he hadn't kissed in a while. But that wasn't the right answer.

First, he wiped his eyes and then answered, "I'm going back over there." He pointed toward Laura. "And you, your son, and Monica should continue your time together."

"So you go back to Laura?"

"So I go back to being a manager. Laura and I are good friends, but I'm not dating anyone. Right now my focus is on searching for Sara and Veronica, being Jere's father, and running this club."

"What about us?"

"Kate, you divorced me!"

"You weren't holding me like we were divorced."

In a voice that was soft and a bit shaky, he said, "No, I was holding you like you were the love of my life." Again, tears came to his eyes.

In a soft, sensual voice, she whispered, "Jack, I want to sleep with you tonight."

Her brown eyes were beautiful, and there was a longing in them. He wanted her too. This was the love of his life sitting next to him. But he couldn't let her back into his life for one night. It would be too painful for her to leave again. "Kate, I want that more than you know, but I'm the man you divorced last year."

"You didn't put up much of a fight."

"I didn't want to live with someone who didn't want me around."

She leaned into his face, almost kissing him. "I want you tonight."

"It would be so easy for me to say yes. But that's only a short answer for a bigger problem. I don't want anyone for one night. Where will you be tomorrow?"

His question startled her. Kate had been acting very sensual, but now she stopped acting, took his hand, and answered his tough question. "I'm not sure, Jack." She knew he was making sense in her head, but emotionally, she didn't want him to go. She raised his hand to her lips and softly kissed it.

"I know that. You'll have to decide that you want me tomorrow, next week, and next year. Kate, I'm not the same person I was a year ago. I'm not going back to being the Jack Fitzgerald of FGNY again. He wasn't bad, but he's not me now. Whatever I do, there would be plenty of time for you, but could you live with me if I didn't move back to New York? I told myself I'd give this search two years. After that, I'd like to find the answers to the questions we're asking tonight." Both had tears filling their eyes. They were being honest with each other, speaking in a closeness they hadn't had in years.

Kate knew Jack would not be coming over tonight, but she still wanted some time with him. "Would you have lunch with us tomorrow if I stayed a couple more days?"

"I can do that. Sure."

She kissed him on the cheek and whispered, "I do love you."

As he rose to leave, she slid her other hand over to hold his hand with both hands. Gently, he slid his hand out and walked away, not turning around. Kate was glad he didn't, because a shiver went through her body from head to toe. She loved this man with every ounce of her soul and had to figure out how to get him back into her life.

Laura had been watching Jack dance with the wrong person. She could tell he was in love with Kate by the many things he did without thinking. He held her naturally. Kate liked being held by Jack, the man she had divorced. She was in love with Jack, this man she had divorced. The two had moved as one. Laura wondered if Kate was stupid or brain-dead. She was in love with Jack, but she had sent him packing.

When Jack returned, Laura tried to be cool about it. "Who was that Jack dancing out there? I've never seen him before."

"I didn't know I could do that. Monica taught Kate what to do, and I've been watching it for several months. It just sort of came together."

"You guys move well together." She wanted to say he danced with the wrong person. Her voice gave her away.

"Yes, but let's not go there tonight." Jack saw the tears in her eyes and knew why. He had mixed feelings. He loved the Kate of his past and Laura. He couldn't believe he just admitted it. "Okay. She's the mother of my children and I love her, but I'm not going back to my old New York lifestyle."

"Uh-huh. But?"

"But I'm not deciding anything right now. I told her that I'm looking for a couple of girls, running this club, and being a father to Jere. After our search has concluded, then I'll tackle some of these other things."

"Okay." Then Laura moved away from Jack. If she stood next to him any longer, she might say what was on her mind. She was wondering how Kate could have let him walk out of her life. He was everything she was looking for and more. She thought, *I love him when he opens the door for me. I love him when he treats me like a real lady. I love to have him touch my shoulder and guide me through the door. When he talks to me, it's with me, and I'm his. I love him because he's honest and honorable.* Laura's eyes filled with tears as she spoke to no one.

Letti had gone to the club to borrow some money, when she found her mother in a daze. "Mom, are you okay?"

"Of course, I am."

"Mom, your eyes were all glassy, like you were in love or something." She had done it again. Letti could read her mother like a map.

Then she saw it was true by her mother's expression. "Mom. You're in love?" Then Letti realized with whom. "You're in love with the big gringo?"

"Hush, girl. He'll hear you."

"Oh my god."

Kate woke up early and alone. She had the finest that money could buy. Her suite in the Hilton lacked nothing. She reached out her arm as if hoping Jack would be there, but she was alone again. She closed her eyes and wrapped her arms around her pillow, remembering the night before. She and Jack danced like when they first dated. He held her, and she knew love. Sex was a needed biological orgasm, but she knew love when Jack held her. Even thinking about it now gave her goose bumps. Back in New York, she was a powerful broker working with billions of dollars. In Cancun, she was in love and alone. She was in love with the man she divorced because she had wanted to live a lifestyle that was no longer attractive to him.

She would have to decide if she wanted love or power and prestige. Her Jack looked great. Mexico was agreeing with him. He seemed alive again and full of fire. Or was it something else? He and Laura seemed very close. Maybe he was falling in love with this Mexican. This meant Kate was not going back to New York for a few more days. This new development meant she would have to decide sooner rather than later if she truly wanted Jack back. Later might be too late.

Anne Saad had been on Jack's staff and stayed to work with Kate. Both had liked the other before Anne started working for Kate. Part of Kate's success was Anne's ability to turn a crisis into a positive experience. Now friends, they spoke frankly about most matters.

"Hello, Anne."

"Hi, Kate. How's Cancun?"

"That's what I'm calling about. I'm going to stay a little longer. My son and I had a great time. He has a girlfriend. I just need to stay a little longer."

"Okay. What are you not saying? You're not saying how good Jack looks! He's probably tanned and so damned good-looking you just can't take your eyes off him!"

"Are we talking about the man I divorced? Why would he interest me now?"

"The same reason he's always interested you. But if you're not interested in him, then maybe I'll fly down and see if he'll take me to dinner."

"Only if you have another job lined up somewhere else."

"Tell me what he looks like now."

"Do you have a crush on him?"

"Honey, he's the hottest man on the planet, and he's single. I've always had a crush on him. I'm sure that no ladies down in Mexico have noticed how handsome he is."

"There's one, Laura. But I don't think Jack's thinking very much about anything else except finding Sara. But Laura's here, and I'm not."

"But you will be for a few more days."

"Right! Let Maggie know. The staff at the house should probably take a week off."

"I'll tell them. Have a good time."

Adnan was just a few months away from leaving Balta for good. He and his son, Ali, were in Singapore to buy school clothes. But while Ali played his video games, Adnan was meeting with some of his other pirate friends in the House of Bathes. In the baths, he enjoyed the pleasures of the ladies, but his real reason was to meet with his new partners. His new company was up and running. He had already transferred five tankers over to the Eastern Green Sea Shipping Corporation. During the last five years, Adnan had stolen millions from Ibrahim, including five tankers.

Adnan planned to send the *Verdi Mare* out one more time for Ibrahim. But after that, she would be anchored in Singapore, where his headquarters was located. He already had Hassan ready to step in for Maged. Maged would have an accident on this last trip, and Hassan would take over as captain.

Carlos Borego was another pirate Adnan had trusted to set up the spin-off company. Everything was in place, except for the tankers waiting to dock. While Adnan was away, Carlos ran everything. Soon though, Adnan would be living in Singapore.

Ibrahim knew about Singapore, and Adnan was just playing into Ibrahim's hands. If Adnan had asked Ibrahim for part of the company, Ibrahim would have given it to him. Ibrahim would also reward his treachery.

It was noon, and Laura was preparing to open the club. She was wearing a Spirit Club T-shirt and a short denim skirt. She was beautiful and sexy for her midforties. Laura had decided to leave the Spirit Club. She had decided Jack was a fool for trying to hang on to something that wasn't there. Kate had divorced him, and he was still meeting her for lunch. Laura was leaving the club, but not without a kiss. Jack owed her that much.

As she walked up to Jack, he knew that something was on her mind and that she was about to get it off. He only hoped it wasn't too bad.

"Jack, you are divorced from this woman? Are you not?"

"Yes." He knew a loaded question when he heard one.

"You are going to meet with her now. Yes?"

"Yes. I'm meeting her and Jere."

With a swift and graceful move, Laura sat on his lap, facing him. She put her arms around his neck and brought him close. He didn't resist. "I love you the way you are. I don't want to change you. But after I kiss you, I quit."

Jack had no time to resist. She not only kissed him, but he also participated. They kissed long and hard with their bodies pressed together. Her heart was racing, and she felt like pulling off her clothes. But she pushed away from the man she loved, stood, turned, and walked away. She was weak and trembling as she walked away, but she kept walking. Laura had decided she could no longer pretend she didn't love him. He wouldn't see the tears. She walked out onto the beach and kept walking.

Laura had come to terms with Veronica's disappearance. There was no hope of finding her. She had stayed at the club because of Jack. As she remembered her moment of passion with Jack, she trembled again. He was going off to meet up with his ex, and they would reconnect. Her head and her heart were fighting. Her head was saying, *Forget about how it felt kissing him. You have left him for good. Now find someone who will love you back.* Meanwhile, her heart was saying, *Go back to the Spirit Club so you can be close to the man you love.* She had reached home too quickly. She couldn't face anyone or talk to anyone right now, so she kept walking.

She still tasted his lips and could remember his kiss. It wasn't the kiss of someone going off to meet the one they loved. He had kissed her back. She paused at an outdoor bar.

In Spanish, she heard "What do you need, lady?"

That was easy enough to answer. "I need Jack."

The bartender dropped a couple of cubes in a glass and poured in two hits of Jack.

Jack sat there for several minutes. He needed Laura in the Spirit Club. *No*, he corrected himself. He wanted Laura to keep working at the Spirit Club. But for now, he needed to be Jere's father. He looked into the mirror and saw a mixed-up Jack. His life with Kate was over. Yes, he loved her, but not her lifestyle. That same lifestyle had been his, but not any longer. The long and short of it was that they were both grasping at shadows of what had once been.

Jack was about to go and meet up with Kate and Jere, but his mind was on a kiss, an embrace. He liked being around Laura. They teased each other and made each other laugh. He liked her pressing hard up against him as they kissed. She had awakened a passion for her that Jack had been trying to deny. But she quit. She was gone.

He and Jere would spend the next couple of days with Kate. Jack would remarry her if she was willing to leave New York, but he was not going back there. He thought he might just stay in Cancun. There were several interesting attractions, including Laura.

When Kate greeted Jack, she realized he was distracted. "Jack, what's wrong?"

"Laura just quit. She'll be hard to replace."

Kate saw a lot more than Jack was willing to admit to her. "I'm sorry."

"Let's go and check out the Mayan pyramid, Chichen Itza. Monica said she can get us there and probably back."

"Probably, Jack?" Kate was hoping for more assurance than "probably."

Jere couldn't tell, but Kate knew Jack was hiding his feelings for Laura. There was a distance that separated them. If she didn't move quickly, the man in her dreams would be her ex forever. If she wanted to connect with Jack, it would have to be soon. Time was on Laura's side.

Jere saw his mom and dad together and not fighting. For Jere, this was enough. He loved them both and was glad peace had been restored. Later, after Kate had returned to her hotel, Jere asked, "What's with you and Mom?"

"Do you mean are we patching things up and getting back together?"

"Well, yeah."

"Do you think your mom's going to move out of her house and come down here?"

"Okay, but at least you're talking."

"Son, just as soon as your mother gets home, she's going to call down here and try and get me to come back for just a visit."

"So that you'll see what you've been missing?"

"I might or might not go, but I won't stay. Your mother loves her lifestyle and New York more than me. Now that's okay. I don't like it, but that's reality. She sorta realizes it, but she'll still call."

"Dad, you're so bad." Then Jere hugged his father, and they both laughed.

Noe had finally put together the missing girls, Jack, and Kate. Now he just had to figure out how to profit from it. He hadn't made the connection until Kate had come to visit Jack Allen and the Spirit Club. A search had pulled up their divorce and income, but here they were together. The other missing girl was Veronica Santos, whose mother was working at the Spirit Club. A man would buy a club just to find his little girl. Noe didn't know how, but he knew he could make a lot of money with this case.

The Santos girl was nothing, but the Fitzgerald girl could prove to be a gold mine. There are two ways for this to happen. One, the father pays big dollars for her safe return, or at least, attempted safe return. Also, he could be rewarded with another promotion. If he were in charge of the police on the strip, he would become very rich. With a lot of money, you can make even more money.

Noe was dreaming of setting up a large organized crime syndicate with Cancun as its headquarters. Maybe he could become powerful enough to become governor. Everything rides on finding out more about this Fitzgerald girl.

On the flight back to JFK, Kate began plotting how she might get Jack back to New York for a visit. He seemed distracted in Cancun. The Laura lady had quit and was no longer a problem. But there was something keeping Jack from really trusting her and being fully hers. She wasn't sure she wanted to move to Mexico or anywhere else, but those questions would only have to be answered if Jack wanted to be with her. If he returned to New York, she knew she could get him into bed, and after that, she would have her man back.

Ann was at JFK, waiting on her boss to arrive. Ann's job was on the line. If Kate stopped working and moved to Mexico, Ann would have to find another cushy job. She worked hard and loved doing what she did. She needed to do whatever she could to help her boss stay happy and with the company. Thus, Ann had brought roses and the limo. They met up in the baggage claim area. Ann bowed, holding out the flowers. "Your humble servants await your every command."

"Ann, I can't have you acting this way. Never mind. I'll just fire you. Be off."

"Bitch."

"There's my Ann. What is all of this stuff?"

"I don't want you to move to Mexico."

"Get real. I'm not moving anywhere."

"But the Mexican beauty was challenging you for Jack."

"If Jack wants me, then he'll just have to move back to New York." Both ladies knew bull when they heard it. But Kate had to sound tough.

"So we have to figure out how to get him back to New York, huh?"
"Absolutely!"

Jack was glad Kate was gone for now. He was glad she had visited, but she was still pushing him in a direction he didn't want to go. He knew she wanted him back in New York, being the old Jack again. But that Jack was gone. She had wanted him to say they could get back together, but he couldn't say that at this point. With Kate gone, so was that pressure.

Al Rendon passed through customs and walked out to find a van going back into town. Vans carried several people for half the price of a taxi. He would need to make his money last. His life had not really been going forward since his last visit. Sara had a hold on him, and she wouldn't let go. He would stay a week or so and figure out how to get rid of her ghost. He had reservations at the Buena Vistas. He was using a friend's time-share, but only for seven days. Then he would have to figure something else out.

On the ride back onto the strip, a smile creased his face. He liked Cancun, and he was glad Sara had brought him back. It was still very hot, but he would put up with the heat to enjoy the view.

Ronnie and Sara had become sisters. At times, they acted like a married couple. One never went very far without the other. Both were beautiful but opposites. As dark as Ronnie was, Sara was light. Ronnie liked to sleep in, while Sara got up with the sun. Sara had blond hair, and Ronnie's was black. Still they loved each other and kept each other hoping.

"What did you think of my Cancun?"

"I loved it up until the moment Rick drugged me away."

"Did you find anyone special?"

"I had several guys hit on me."

"But was there a guy that you wanted to talk to?"

"There was one, but I only remember his first name, Al. He wasn't tall or dark or handsome. He was just nice. I laughed with him. We didn't laugh at anyone. We just laughed. He was there that night, but he wouldn't come over. I guess he felt I was too young or something. I would like to see him again."

"So how many children will you give him?"

"Ronnie!" Then Sara hit her with a pillow. And for a little while, they forgot they were prisoners on an island somewhere.

After a while, Sara said she wanted to go for a walk alone. Ronnie thought it was a little funny but let her friend go.

In the morning, Ronnie came into the living room. She saw Sara sitting on the sofa, crying. "What do you think about virginity?"

"I'm certainly not one."

"Well, me either now." Then Sara pointed to her lips for Ronnie not to talk. She pointed to the walls and then her ears, meaning *they are probably listening.* Then she reached into the sofa and pulled out a telescope.

"Listen, girl, let's walk to the hotel for some coffee." Ronnie knew they had coffee, but she wanted to talk to Sara about the telescope.

"Sounds fine by me. I'm glad you finally got up." They both faked laughing.

When it felt safe, Ronnie asked, "What the hell did you do?"

"I got us a telescope to look out at the sea. I don't know what we'll find, but I needed to do something."

"You'd never had sex before?"

"I'd come close, but no. I didn't have sex last night. He did. I was just a body."

"Oh, Sara, I'm sorry."

"Well, they track our money, so I paid for it a different way."

"Who with?"

"I'm sorry, Ronnie, I'm not telling. Every time you saw him, you'd stare. If I'm found out, then you aren't in trouble, neither is he."

"So you just said to a guy, 'Hey, I'll do it for a telescope'?"

"We talk off and on. One day he told me he had a telescope at home, and he liked watching stars and ships and other things. Then I talked him into sneaking it onto the island. He suggested the sex part, and I finally agreed."

"Where?"

"There's a room they use for briefings and training. It had a couch in it. I don't want to talk about it anymore. Except we'll be able to look at stars, ships, and stuff."

Beginning that evening, Sara began looking at stars, ships, and stuff.

Kate woke up hugging her pillow. She had just been dreaming about Cancun. She remembered Jack holding her and the two of them dancing like they had a long time ago. She hugged him again, using the pillow. Whether or not Jack came to visit her, she would be returning to Cancun. With that thought, a little piece of electricity ran through her body. "Jack, you've still got it."

It was time to speak with Laura. Jack missed her and wanted her around.

"Hello, Mr. Jack."

"Hi, Letti. Is your mom home?"

"She's not home to you. Those are her words."

"I thought as much. Just tell her this will be my last phone call unless she comes by to see me. I don't want to bother or harass her. Oh, also, tell her I love her. Bye."

Fifty-three minutes later, Laura came by the club to see Jack. She came bouncing in as if she had never left. "*Ola*, Jack. What did you tell my daughter?" Her eyes were almost penetrating him.

Jack went and got two glasses and a bottle of Jack. He poured some Jack into both glasses. Then he dropped in a couple of cubes and topped them with Coke. "Have a seat. This won't be a short story." Then he handed her a drink.

"In about a week, I expect my ex to call down here, demanding that I go up to New York for some very good reason. I'll have to go, and then she'll wave my old life in front of me again, trying to entice me back into it. It won't work, and then I'll tell her goodbye for good. Down here, I'm in love with a Mexican maiden who has stolen my heart. I love everything about her. Except I can't tell her that until the mother of my son cuts me loose once and for all. I feel obligated to marry her again if she were willing to come down here and live with me and her son. I am not going back to New York to live. I might not stay in Cancun, but I know that I'm not going back to New York.

"You see, I love this one Mexican lady very much, but I couldn't tell her that yet until this other thing gets settled. Well, that Mexican lady pushed and pushed, and so now I have to tell her ahead of schedule that I love her."

One more time, Laura jumped up and ran and straddled Jack. They kissed for a long time. Jack broke free and said, "You didn't give me a chance to tell you the name of the Mexican lady."

"Shut up and kiss her!"

Both were hungry for sex and love. They kissed, tasting that thing they had lost. Jack loved the feel of Laura's small frame pressed hard against his. He was hungry for sex with the right person, and she was the right person. He tasted her ear and moved down her neck. Then they kissed again.

Laura couldn't believe she was sitting on her gringo's lap. He was kissing her, and she knew she wanted to taste him and feel him next to her. This was too good. She felt alive and young and tingling. Her heart was pounding as he moved from her lobe to her nape. Then he moved closer to her breast and then back to her mouth. Laura's whole body was on fire!

Jack's passion was about to explode when he pushed her away. Jack held up his hands as if he were under arrest. "We can't do this right now."

With eyes wide-open, she stared at him. "I think I can. I'll lock the door."

"Laura, that's not what I mean. What I mean is that I love you, but we shouldn't have sex right now, today."

She could have had sex right then. She didn't understand him. Her body was saying right now was the perfect time. "You mean because we are supposed to open soon?"

"No, because I mean you are not my wife yet."

Again her eyes came wide-open as she ran to him. "Can you explain that 'yet' to me?"

That night, Jere came up to Jack. "Hey, Dad, how'd you get her to come back?"

"I bought her a drink, and we had a long talk. I told her I needed her help with this place."

"Sure, Dad. Whatever you say." Jere knew his dad liked Laura, and that was cool.

It had taken a day for Al to build up his courage to return to the Spirit Club. He came back on Friday and now Saturday. Several ladies had been looking at him, and a few had offered to buy him drinks. Al had just been watching life at the Spirit Club and not participating. Another young blonde came up and offered to buy him a drink. Reluctantly, he turned her down. Before he could dance or drink with anyone else, he would have to figure out how to get rid of the ghost of Sara. It would probably mean a visit to the police station.

Pedro couldn't help himself when he saw Al turn away another pretty girl. "Mister, they don't come any prettier than that one. I don't know what you're waiting for."

"I know you're right, but I'm just not ready to let go of a blonde that I met here last year. The next person that offers to buy me a drink, I'm going to accept."

Laura had been listening in on their conversation, so she offered. "Hello, cowboy, I'd like to buy you that next drink."

"Sure, why not."

"Pete, give him whatever he wants. It's nice to meet you. I'm Laura Santos from Cancun. Can we sit down at a table?"

Laura made Al feel comfortable. He didn't believe she was after his body, so he would enjoy a conversation with this older Mexican beauty. "Is this your club?"

"No. I just work here. Ownership changed hands last year, and I started working here then. An American who looks and talks like a Mexican?"

"I'm from Austin, Texas. I'm a native Texan. That makes us *primos*."

"I guess so. How long are you here for?"

"I've rented a cabana on the beach for seven days."

"Where's your date?"

"Does this mean you are not my date?"

"You are handsome, but I have my eye on someone a little older."

"I don't have a date. I was here last year and found someone I wanted to get to know better, but that didn't happen."

"The blonde I heard you talking to Pete about?"

"Yes. I had to come back and just remember."

"Maybe I've seen her. Describe her for me."

"She was blond and about 5'5". She had just finished high school. She was perky and happy. Her name was Sara. I didn't get a last name."

Laura's hand began to shake as she reached into her purse for Sara's photo. Now a year later, they might have their first real clue as to what happened.

Al couldn't believe his luck. Laura had a picture of his Sara. "This is unbelievable! That's Sara. Oh my god! I can't believe it." His hand came up to his mouth. He hugged Laura. "Where is she?"

"Come with me." Laura knew Jack was working in the office.

When Laura walked in with Al, Jack knew something was up, but he had no idea what.

Laura didn't make him wonder long. "Hi, Jack. This is Al from Texas. Al, meet Jack, the manager of the Spirit Club." Nods and handshakes were exchanged.

"Al, would you tell Jack why you came back to Cancun?"

"Sure. I came back because I was haunted by a memory of Sara."

Jack's eyes grew wide as he heard his daughter's name. Jack could barely speak, but he told Al, "Go on."

"Sir, I met your daughter here about a year ago."

Trying to cover up his excitement, Jack asked, "What makes you think she is my daughter?"

"If we're being honest, it was your eyes. Right now, they grew wide like you had just seen a ghost. But also, they're her eyes."

"Go ahead."

"We spoke briefly the night before, but I wanted to know her better, so I returned. Her friends seemed to pair off with other guys, so I started over toward her. A guy by the name of Rick cut me off at the pass. He had a drink in his hand for her, but I saw her glance at me. My hope was that she would talk with him for a minute and then it would be my turn. I waited a few minutes, but she and Rick got up and left.

"I wasn't comfortable with the situation. Rick seemed to be helping her out the door. I wondered if she had left on her own, so I started for the door. It was very dark because it was raining. I didn't see them at first, but then I saw them round a corner. As I moved forward, everything went black. When I woke up, I had a bad headache, and my wallet and shoes were gone.

"Someone had clubbed me. I was robbed, but I'm not sure that was the reason for stopping me. I guess I'm back here talking to you because Sara is missing?"

"That's good, Al. You're right. No one saw Sara after that night."

"Sir, I started to go to the police, but my ship was sailing that afternoon. I had no ID, so I just went back to my ship. We sailed on up to Canada, and I finished my contract with that company and returned to Texas. I used that money to work on a master's at UT in Austin. I never stopped thinking about Sara. She's the kind of girl you want to be with. I knew so little about her, and I wanted to know more."

"Listen, Al, I do want you to talk to the police, but we'll bring the police captain to you, okay?" Jack and Al visited a long time that Saturday night. For Jack, it was like visiting with his daughter.

On Sunday evening, Captain Sanchez visited the Buena Vista condos. "Mr. Rendon?"

"Yes, Captain, come in. Mr. Allen said you'd be coming by."

"It grieves me that we can't do this at the station, but I have some problems there. Enough. Now tell me about Sara and this Rick."

"Rick is about five feet ten. He's blond with a medium build. Maybe American . . ."

"Al, this is a very interesting story. I think our little ladies were, in fact, kidnapped. I'll need to send a sketch artist to you so we can figure out what this Rick looks like. We can do this tomorrow, okay?"

"Sure. Thanks, and goodbye." Not being ready to turn in, Al went over to the Spirit Club.

Christi watched everything from her VW. The bug went on the expense account and would stay with Mr. Allen after all this was over. Once again, the same girl, Maria Longoria, had followed the captain to the Buena Vistas. She watched as the captain left. Maria stayed to follow Al to the Spirit Club.

When Al got to the Spirit Club, Christi was there to meet him. "Hi, I'm Christi. I work for Mr. Allen, and you're being followed. She's probably going to hit on you to find out what you were talking to the captain about."

"What the hell are you talking about?"

"Why didn't you go to the station?"

"I'm not sure I should be telling you anything."

"That's a good answer. I'm investigating Sara's disappearance. My job today was to watch your place. Maria followed the captain to Buena Vistas and then followed you here. She's going to come in and hit on you to get information from you about why you are here. Your answer is that you are looking for work and Mr. Allen offered you a job."

"Has he?"

"He will tonight."

"I'm going to the ladies' room, and then I will sit somewhere else. Bye." Christi was thirty-three and loved to tease and have fun. She threw her hips as she walked to the ladies' room. Some older ladies might have wrenched a back muscle or something else swinging as hard as she was. I guess men swagger and women swing those hips.

As if on cue, Maria entered the Spirit Club. For Al, it seemed like she was missing the muted trumpet playing some sexy swing music. She was swinging, and her prey sat in plain sight. Soon she would have him eating out of her hand. Men are always looking for a woman to bed. She would make it easy for this one, and then he would tell her anything she wanted to know, just for a little more amour. She headed for the ladies' room. Maria passed Christi coming out of the restroom as she went in.

Christi knew that Maria would be pushing up her breasts, touching up her lips, and applying a little scent. Maria was also raising the slit in her skirt. Her skirt had a zipper for such occasions. Now she was barely legal with her tanned thigh exposed.

Maria sat down between the dance floor and Al. He couldn't look at those dancing without spying her. She sat so that the slit was exposed. Her blouse was thin and open. In fact, she looked like many of the ladies in the club. Finally, she caught him looking in her direction, so she crossed her leg, exposing a little more skin.

Laura saw the trap and moved to sit in front of his view, blocking out Maria. "You are the fly, and she is the spider."

"Does everyone know what's going on, except for me?"

"That's Maria. She works for Noe, a dirty cop. He's the number 2 guy out here on the strip. The guy that was number 2 before him had an 'accident,' if you know what I mean. Now all that stands between him and ripping off all these hotels and clubs is the captain. Noe works on both sides of the law. When it suits him, he looks the other way and then turns around with his hand out. She's going to want to know why you are here. You are here applying for a job."

"Mr. Allen's going to hire me?"

"Right now. Let's go."

Al took a job as a manager trainee. The word circulating said he had been brought down from up north. Al had applied for the job through the offices of the corporation headquarters in New York. Victor would sign off on that, and Kim would write a letter notifying Jack that Al was coming to interview for the job. Alfredo Rendon could not afford to live at the Buena Vistas, but his boss could afford it. So Al would stay put. Next they would need to get him transportation and a work visa. Money would take care of the transportation, and the captain would help with the visa.

Monday,
OCTOBER 1, 2001

With the team all together, the *Verdi Mare* set sail for the port of Cancun. The ship would not go directly to Cancun. It needed to pick up some Russian-made weapons in Istanbul. Then Maged would take his tanker through Suez and pick up the weapons. Next he would head to Libya to drop off the weapons for diamonds and gold. The diamonds and gold had come from Ethiopia and the Sudan. Next he would get a great price for the gold and diamonds in Venezuela for some cheap oil. Finally, he would pick up some propane in Matamoros. In Cancun, his crew could relax for a few days while they also picked up another lady.

Onboard the ship, Maged was the only person loyal to Ibrahim, and Adnan planned to replace him along the way. The *Verdi Mare* would only stop at Balta on the way back. She would drop off one new captive, and then she was off to her new home, Singapore.

Maged didn't feel good about the trip. He was the captain of a ship that would be picking up one more girl. For him, it would be the last. Ibrahim knew he was retiring after this trip. Maged knew he should have never made the first trip, but here he was, making one more. Money and fear help a person decide important matters in their lives. He was afraid of Ibrahim, and he liked his money. Morally, he could blame it on the fear, but he knew he was going for the money he would make.

He would not be going to Florida, where his family was. His girls were married now, and his wife, well, she was financially taken care of. He would go off and live on an island where he would be waited on, hand and foot. His money would be in a Swiss account, so the politics of the island wouldn't matter. But first, he had to get one more girl from Cancun back to Balta. It was time for vodka.

Ibrahim called a family meeting, normally done once a year. He hugged all the grandkids and then let them go off and play. With only his sons and daughters in the room, he told them that he and Saad were going sailing and would be gone for a few weeks. "I've called you together to tell you all at the same time that Saad and I are going to sea. I plan to be gone two weeks out and two weeks back. If we are having a good time, then we might stay longer. While I'm gone, Adnan will continue to run the shipping business. Ben will continue to take care of the casino. Of course, Rebecca will run the school. Yosef will have my power of attorney over everything. We will be on satellite phone, so we will always be in touch."

Ben spoke for the family. "Don't worry about us. We will be okay. Have a good time and enjoy the sea."

"Thank you, Ben. Now let's eat." Ben felt like his father was saying goodbye. He knew they wouldn't be getting back home in a month. At least, it would be several months, if at all. He went along with his father's game just the same.

Adnan was there to see Ibrahim off. He'd no idea that Ibrahim was leaving until word was sent to prepare the yacht. He wanted only a small crew, and they would be gone for four or five weeks. Adnan had many questions, but he was afraid to talk to Ibrahim. He had watched Ibrahim kill before, and he wanted to stay away from him. He didn't trust himself. He thought he might betray his plans, so it was better to stay away from Ibrahim. "Ibrahim, peace be with you, and have a good and safe trip. May Allah protect you."

"Adnan, we don't believe in God. If we did, we should have lived differently."

Adnan wasn't sure what had just transpired, but he wondered if there hadn't been a coded message there.

Saad didn't speak at all. He just carried his bag and went on board. Then the yacht sailed out of port. Ibrahim was off the island. Adnan needed to find out where they were really going. Ben might know.

As the yacht left, Ibrahim checked in with his number 2. "We have supplies for two months?"

"Yes, and I also took care of the New York problem."

"Good. Let's enjoy our time now." Only Saad was from Balta. Three other single men came from Bird Island to finish off his crew.

Frank, like many Americans, was not the same anymore. The events of 9/11 had changed his priorities. He had decided to retire from the company. In the last twelve months, he had earned five million, but now he just wanted to leave New York City and have family around. He already had more money than he could possibly ever spend. Someone would need to replace him, and that someone was currently in Mexico.

"Hello, Jack. This is Frank. Got a minute?"

"Sure. What's up?"

"Can I come down and visit with you? I'm rolling some ideas around in my head, and I just want to know what you think about them."

"Sure. If you want, Victor can fly you down, or just hop on a plane. Call me when you decide."

"All right, we'll talk soon. Thanks."

Jack was bothered by the phone call. Frank was probably ready to hang it up. But what would they be discussing? Jack had started the company, but Frank had been a great pickup. He'd been tired of working for others and wanted to buy into Jack's company. They had been great partners until Jack no longer wanted to play the game. Could Frank be planning to talk him into going back? They'd have to wait and see.

Johnny Trudle had been working on the case for more than a year and was very close to the truth. The island of Balta was a private island with a casino and a shipping business on it. Several of the workers lived on Bird Isle, but no one talked. Balta was an independent island state, much like Monaco. It wasn't part of Indonesia, but Indonesia protected it.

Johnny had been on Bird Isle for just over a month. He didn't look like the locals, but they had stopped staring at him. He wasn't really accepted, but he was becoming more familiar day by day. Today Johnny just milled around and fished. After a while, he fished some and milled around. Actually, he was pretty boring, so people stopped watching him. He was a stray, but he wasn't hurting anything and he paid his bills, so he was left alone.

He had hired a guide, Abdul-Rahmon whom he called Raymond because he couldn't say the other name, to take him out into deeper waters to fish. Today they were about to go out fishing when Johnny saw a big tanker leaving Balta.

"I guess they come and go a lot?"

"Yes, a lot."

"What's her name?" Johnny was squinting, trying to read the name. He couldn't see it at all, but he acted like he was guessing. "*Verdi*. Does it say *Verdi*?"

"Nope. That is the *Black Duck*. The *Verdi* left two days ago."

"How do you know that?"

"Johnny, my brother works over there. But we don't talk about stuff like that. He just happened to tell me. Mr. Ibrahim pays pretty good, but if he finds out you talk, he'll kill you. So nobody talks."

Johnny was thinking that someone would know where the *Verdi Mare* was sailing.

Suddenly, there was a monstrous blast. The building that Johnny had been renting flew apart. There was a white flash that filled the dock. What had been calm and peaceful was now white and loud. Those standing on the dock were thrown into the water like paper dolls. As Johnny flew through the air, he crashed into a board coming from the opposite direction or flying in his direction. Everything went black. Raymond flew with him. A small car crashed into Raymond in midair.

Thursday,
OCTOBER 4, 2001

F rank came to work only to tie up some loose ends and then leave. He would be leaving his assistant, Steve Cook, in charge. He stopped by to see Kate, just to say he was taking two days off and he would see her on Monday. He stopped to visit with Victor to get a reading on whether or not Jack would return.

"Enjoy Cancun, Frank, because Jack won't be coming back."

"Well, I'll try. I miss him, and we'll have a good visit." With that, Frank was off to JFK for a three-hour flight to Cancun.

Adnan was really worried by Ibrahim's departure. He decided he and Carlos needed to visit Cancun. They would fly instead of traveling on his tanker. Adnan needed Carlos's knowledge of Spanish for his visit. Adnan wasn't sure what was happening, but he wanted to get closer to the action. If Ibrahim wound up in Cancun, maybe Adnan could dispose of his problem there, but first, he needed to go to Singapore to pick up Carlos. Adnan also sent his family on a vacation to Singapore to get them away from the island that had been their only home.

Ibrahim had his sloop swing by Louis Island to pick up his good friend Dr. Hung. Ibrahim was feeling weaker and wanted to talk with the doctor about his condition. Doc needed some sea time anyway. Ibrahim greeted him in the Arabic tradition, with three kisses. They had been pirates together for a long time, and they truly liked each other. Pirates can only trust a few people without having them turn on them, and Hung was one of those. Hung's father had sailed with Ibrahim's father. He settled on Louis Island, and his three children still lived there. Hung was single again, so he could go with his good friend Ibrahim. For Hung, the trip was not a surprise. Ibrahim had been talking about it since his last visit to Louis Island.

"Hello, my friend. Peace be with you."

"So you have come to get a second opinion on your cancer?"

"Yes and no. I believe my doc, but I thought it time to begin a new chapter in my life. Also, you might have some ideas on how to extend my time."

"Ibrahim, there are many things we can do and maybe many places we should visit one more time."

"We have shared much, my friend."

With that said, Hung had his supplies brought on board the *Minnie Mae*. Ibrahim had named his yacht the *Minnie Mae*. His first love had been a nurse who died when they were both young and in love. Her name was Minnie Majorichkova. He had shortened it to just Minnie Mae. They were in love in Jakarta where she worked on the ship *Hope*. She caught hepatitis C working in the hospital there and died too young. She had just wanted to help people live a better life. Her dream took her from Ibrahim. Now she was just a sweet memory.

Christi walked into the Spirit Club with red eyes. She announced, "Johnny's dead."

The office went silent.

"What are you talking about?"

"Johnny always listed me as next of kin, and I was just called from Bird Island, near Indonesia. An official said that there was an explosion and Johnny was killed. I need to go there and get him. Can we use the jet?"

"I'm sorry, Christi. Yes, of course, you can use the jet. I'll call Victor, and it will be here tomorrow."

"No. I need to fly to Newark." Christi's world suddenly changed. Her best friend was now dead. The teen was still missing. For the first time in many months, she was lost. A fog settled over her, and she had trouble seeing. She knew Johnny's wife, Pat, needed to be called, but not yet. How could Johnny actually be dead?

Laura didn't say anything. She just walked over and held Christi. Christi held on and cried. Laura stayed with her awhile. Jack knew Johnny had been murdered. He also thought about the two little ladies held by them, the murderers.

He walked into his office and picked up Sara's photo. Jack wondered if she was alive. And what does that mean, *alive*? Did she belong to some small king or pirate? Was she part of a harem? Was she being treated nicely, or was she a slave girl chained to a wall, only released for whatever her master wanted? Jack knew what he wanted for her kidnappers. He was thinking about a lot of pain and then death.

As he looked at the photo, he saw a young Kate. He hoped his daughter had some of him in her, but she looked like a young Kate.

With each passing day, it was less likely he would ever see his Sara again. He cried. "I promise you, Sara, that I will never give up looking for you. You have my word, with God as my witness."

He thought the unreasonable—*what if she is found?* Jack thought that if Jere would come, he would take both of them on an extended vacation. Then he lowered his head and cried softly.

Laura saw him with his head in his hands and knew why he was crying. She took her fingernails and softly scratched his back. But he was lost in a world of sadness. She just sat next to him and held on to his arm. No words were spoken. Laura cried a little for both girls.

From time to time, he would take a deep breath. After a good while, she just walked away from him and kept everyone else away. Today was his hardest day away from Sara. What was her day like?

Laura thought that if they had any chance at all of finding the girls, it was only because Jack had money. If her daughter was found, it would be because Jack had money. Neither his country nor hers was looking for the two young ladies. Laura didn't know if they had even survived the kidnapping. According to Al, Sara had left with Rick. Did he take her to the *Verdi Mare*? Was Veronica already there? Did they get on another ship? Were there more girls taken that night? Laura thought of the bigger picture now. She wondered how many women are taken against their will. Are there hundreds, or even thousands? For now, she could only focus on two.

At the exact moment that Jack promised to never stop looking for her, a cold chill ran through Sara. She looked up and said, "Wow."

Veronica asked, "*Wow* what?"

"I don't know. A cold chill just went through my whole body."

"What do you mean?"

"I don't know what I mean."

"You are one weird girl."

"Does that mean you don't want to go with me when my dad comes for me?"

"I can live with weird. Yes, I want to go with you."

"Cool, just checking."

Later that afternoon, Frank's flight touched down, and a Jack Allen was there to meet him. Jack took him to the Grand Palace Hotel. Jere and Laura joined them for supper. At a distance, Maria took several photos that she knew Noe would want as he pieced together his plan to make money off of the two missing young ladies.

Maged was captain of the ship. He was a pirate, and his crew could not be trusted. Whenever he was outside his quarters on the ship, he was armed. He had no friends aboard, so he stayed in his room most of the time. The last time he saw Ibrahim, he looked a little sick. Maged couldn't quite put his finger on it. Ibrahim had almost treated him like a friend. Ibrahim knew this was Maged's last trip. When he got back to Balta, he would retire. Maged's family lived in Florida and was well taken care of. He wanted to go someplace and have a maid wait on his every need. He wasn't particular. It could be some small isle or perhaps Costa Rica. Now all he had to do was survive this last trip.

The pirates' blood flowed through Ibrahim's veins. It was great to be out at sea on a small ship, only worrying about what was in front of you. He had taken care of the island of Balta for too long. Now he was free of it. Ben would have to deal with all his former issues. Ibrahim had only to deal with the sea. He had a small fortune put away for this day. Money wouldn't be a problem. His final problem was not dealing with his cancer. Rather, it would be dealing with Adnan in Cancun one last time. Ibrahim was following the *Verdi Mare* from in front. He knew her ports of entry and would be there waiting to see what might happen. His crew would watch and report to him.

The irony of the whole situation was that Adnan had stolen what was already his. Ibrahim didn't mind sharing half of the shipping business with Adnan. He got angry as he thought about Adnan betraying not only him but also his father's trust in him. Ibrahim would not hold a grudge, but Adnan would die. He would die knowing that he hadn't stolen anything. Ibrahim would have everything returned to his family. His wives and sons would be on the streets of Singapore with no money, no home, and no Adnan.

Yosef and Ali Al Mutari had called a meeting with Ben. In the meeting, Yosef disclosed that Ibrahim had an inoperable cancer and would not be returning from his trip. He also told Ben that Ibrahim wanted Adnan and his people thrown out of the shipping business. Adnan had been cheating his father for years. It was likely Adnan would murder Ibrahim's whole family if he thought Ibrahim was not returning. Yosef was set for a raid if Ben would give the okay. Ben knew Yosef to be Ibrahim's most trusted friend. There was no hesitation.

"Let's do it!"

Ibrahim had twenty-five special forces–type guards that always protected him and his family. Yosef had the elite guard standing by and ready for a visit to the shipping facility. The raid lasted for about only an hour. There had been some small arms fire exchanged, but the special forces moved in with precision and took over the shipping yard. Adnan's leadership was executed on the spot. The rest had their hands secured behind their backs and were escorted to Bird Isle.

"If you return, we will shoot you on sight! Now go away." They weren't given any monetary assistance. Their unfaithfulness was repaid.

Ali Al Mutari kept a few of the computer/finance people to clean up all of Adnan's deceptions and double-dealings. They were held in cells when not at work. The finance guys had one chance to stay alive. That would be their task of transferring everything back to Ben.

Most of Adnan's workers heeded Yosef's advice. A few didn't. Everything they had in the world had just been taken from them, and they were not ready to give it up just yet. Micah told them there was nothing left for them here. Adnan had promised all of them jobs in Singapore. But first they had to do a little damage to Balta Island to pay back Ali Al Mutari and Yosef.

After breakfast, Frank told Jack why he had come. "Are you ready for the New York city grind again, Jack?"

"Are you kidding me, Frank? Look around. No, I'm never going back there. When I left the company, I had no idea that I would be living in Cancun. I might not stay here, but I'm not going back there."

"I know, Jack. I just wanted to confirm it with your own words. I want to walk away also. But I need to find the right person to replace me. Victor wouldn't do it. He works for you. I've got Steve in charge while I'm gone. He can do it. Kate's been great. She's inventive and smart, but she's not the right person to be in charge of the whole company."

"You could always bring in someone from outside the company."

"I know you don't mean that. We are not just about making money. We did it with integrity. I would need to know the person really well."

"You mean like Steve?"

"So we agree I should offer it to him?"

Jack just smiled.

Christi landed at Newark and then took a taxi to Jersey City to see Pat. When she walked up to Pat's door, Pat was looking out the window. The scene was like a commander coming to a soldier's next of kin to deliver terrible news. Pat knew, but she had to ask, "Where's Johnny?"

Christi had practiced what to say, but it wouldn't come out. She just looked at Pat.

"Don't tell me he's not coming home!" Pat's expression was one of disbelief. Then the tears came. Christi held Pat because Pat needed to be held, but Christi needed to be held too. Pat lost a husband, and Christi lost her best friend.

Christi noticed that Pat had put on a few pounds. As she pulled away, she glanced at her midriff. Pat nodded. "I'm five months, twins." A little happiness mingled with horrible grief. Pat would not be making the trip to pick up Johnny.

Monday,
OCTOBER 8, 2001

Victor, Christi, and a small staff landed on Bird Isle. Americans would have considered the airport rustic. Victor visited with the immigration personnel, and then everyone was allowed to disembark. There wasn't anything like Holiday Inn, but they found rooms to rent. That same afternoon, they met with the officials holding Johnny. Everything he had was lost in the explosion.

Victor was in charge of the trip. Christi was pretty useless. When someone suffers the shock of losing someone close to them, their bodies medicate them. Christi's body had given her a dose, which caused her mind to function in slow motion. Victor's staff worked quickly to complete their gruesome chore of bringing Johnny's body onboard in the storage area. The police had Victor sign for the wallet and keys found on Johnny. There wasn't any cash, but his credit cards all seemed to be there.

"Have you spoken with any witnesses?"

"There are no witnesses. This is a small isle. Even now, we are being watched. If anyone came forward, they would end up like your friend. So we are sure it was a gas leak. The investigation is closed."

"Can we spend the night before taking off?"

"Sir, I would not recommend it, but yes."

All of Johnny's possessions had been blown up. Victor had his wallet and keys. One key was for a safety deposit box. After everyone was settled in, Victor needed to go to the bank.

Not far from where Victor's party was staying, Adnan's workers were preparing to blow up the ships in mooring and as many of the buildings as they could. The attack was intended only to do as much damage as possible, and then they would clear out. Their fun would happen at dusk.

On Balta, security was still at its highest point. Guards were ready for anything that might happen. Sara and Veronica had been told to stay in their condo for two more days. Rebecca told them the former manager of the shipping business had been fired for cheating their father out of billions. But no one knew where he was. They were expecting word from him in the way of an attack. The casino had been emptied, and all was quiet, too quiet.

Adnan was in Singapore, running his new business. Ten of his "friends" were preparing to pay Balta a visit. Speaking to no one, Adnan went into another rage. "How could that stinking pirate betray his closest friend? He will pay for this dearly. Balta Island will be in shambles after tonight, and soon I will kill me a pirate with my own hands."

Later that afternoon, Victor had Christi go with him to the bank. There in a safety deposit box lay a small notebook. Under it was an envelope addressed to Christi.

> Dear Christi, it may sound ironic, but I have loved and trusted you like a sister. I know Pat will see this, and she will have to get over the fact that I put my life in your hands on several occasions. I love Pat as a wife, but you have been a trusted friend. Yes, Pat, I loved you and was always faithful to you. God put us together, and I trusted you completely.
>
> Now, Christi, since you are reading this, the news about me cannot be good. I don't want to die, but I want to catch those monsters who traffic in souls. After finding out about the kidnappings, I would have worked for free to find those evil—I'm not going to put down what they are. Those who think it is okay to kidnap someone make me want to hurt them in the worst way. I'm grateful to Jack for supporting us in our search. Yes, I have info for you, but you need to get off this island right now. Read the notebook in the air. Grab everything and everybody, and leave right now.

That was enough for Victor. "I believe him. Let's get out of here." He quickly gathered everyone and headed to the airport and the jet.

Micah had been the son of a pirate with only a first name. He chose Sinbad as his last name. He had been in contact with Adnan since his expulsion and was placed in charge of the raid. The plan was to do as much damage as possible and then clear out. He was to take no prisoners. He was to kill as many people as he could and blow up as much stuff as he could. The ships just needed a hole in the side and had to be set on fire. Buildings could be burned with mortars.

So the attack began. Three speedboats raced toward the shore of Balta. Ibrahim's forces were as prepared as they could be. Yosef's orders were to take no prisoners. They knew who was behind the attack and would only kill anyone approaching the island. The three speedboats launched twenty-four rockets at the shipping side of Balta. Micah knew they would have to get close to attack the ships at the dock.

By the time the rockets took off, Ibrahim's two combat helicopters were in the air. The three speedboats soon became burning rubble. Micah was a part of the burning rubble. He never got to use his second name. Yosef's own boats went out to kill anyone still alive. He gathered as many bodies as he could. He needed to burn them as well.

The rockets were not powerful, but damage was done. Rebecca's home had taken a direct hit. She was wounded, and two of her children were killed. Outside Sara's condo, a rocket struck a tree and blew out their windows. A few other buildings were on fire. None of the business buildings or equipment were hit. Except for Rebecca's family, nobody had been hurt by the attack. The island had been cleared of everyone except for about a hundred people who had been told to stay indoors. It was loud for a few moments, and then people started on what needed to be done. Fires were put out. Medical aid was given to Rebecca. So far, Ben was not enjoying life as the head pirate.

The notebook only had four entries in it, one for each week Johnny had been there. The entry Victor and Christi were interested in was October 1. This was written in the notebook:

> Today is October 1, 2001. The *Verdi Mare* is moored at
> Balta Island. The owner/king is Ibrahim Al Balta. He

runs a shipping business on the island, and there is a casino operating for those people he does business with. You can only enter the island by invitation. I have not been able to get invited as of today. Of course, these are smart people, and they know that I'm on Bird Isle. The *Verdi Mare* is in dock here, but it is registered to Adnan Kareem of Singapore. He owns the Eastern Green Sea Shipping Inc.

My best guess is that the girls were brought to Balta. Let me just think out loud and then write it down in this notebook. Again, these are only my thoughts, no proof. I wouldn't know if they were dealt to someone else after getting here. If they are still here, I wouldn't have any idea what they are doing for Ibrahim. Again, security is very tight, just like a prison. The girls could be living on the island and be free to move around, but you only come or go with Ibrahim's approval.

Jack, I don't want to get your hopes up, but if the girls stayed here on Balta, then they probably weren't brought here to work on the docks, loading and unloading. The casino seems to be only for his shipping clients. I'm guessing almost all would be males. What attracts all males? Bait. Some girls would be used for prostitution, but the really pretty ones, like our young ladies, would be for show. I would put them around in different places. Of course, I don't know how many he might have, but they could just be used as dolls / eye candy. They would need to live in nice quarters so that they stayed looking nice. It might have cost Ibrahim a million dollars per girl to get them here, so I would think that he'd want to take good care of them. Again, Jack, this is only what I would do if I were this guy.

My reluctant guide is Abdullrahmon. I just call him Raymond. He's probably passing on all information of my activities to Ibrahim. I need to leave as soon as possible and probably sometime this week.

Christi and Victor closed the notebook. They needed to visit with Jack. As they closed the notebook, outside their window was an amazing fireworks display. This Ibrahim was celebrating something.

Adnan hadn't heard from Micah yet. That was not good news. It should have only taken thirty minutes for the raid. Adnan would travel to Cancun on a fake Mexican passport. It might be time to leave before people started looking for him.

Frank went to work late on Monday. He told his secretary, Brenda, to have Steve Cook stop by his office as soon as it was convenient. Frank had a big smile on his face for some reason. Brenda thought Cancun must have agreed with him. Frank hadn't announced he was going to see Jack, but she had made his reservations and knew Jack was there.

The jet landed back in Newark and would stay there as the crew rested, according to FAA rules. Dave Roberts met Victor after they landed. He would take care of all the legal matters pertaining to Johnny and his return. Kate had loaned Tony to drive everyone wherever they needed to go. Kim would do whatever Victor needed her to do, from making phone calls to writing checks. She always carried cash, plastic, and checks. Johnny was transported via hearse to Riotto Funeral Home in Jersey City. The funeral and Mass would be at Holy Rosary Church on Saturday. There would be a Rosary said on Friday when most of Johnny's family and friends would gather. Johnny would be laid to rest next to his sister in Holy Name Cemetery. Her murder was the reason he had gotten into law enforcement, and her husband's murder was the reason he'd left the Jersey City Police Force. Law enforcement had to obey all the legal system's laws, while criminals chose to ignore them. As a private investigator, Johnny could move almost unseen in their world. On Bird Isle, he had been seen, and it had cost him his life.

Jack had stayed in Cancun with his son and would not be there for the funeral. He could not bring Johnny back with his presence, but he might be able to find the girls if he stayed. Al was now part of the group looking for clues. The manager, Dave Hudson, had Al grow a beard to change his appearance.

Jere didn't really know what was happening. It was just another Cancun morning for him and his buddy Alex. Almost every morning, around ten, they would jog a couple of miles up and down the beach. Jere stood 6'5". His hair was a white-bleached blond. His dad was Irish, with dark hair; but he had his mom's blond hair, as did Sara. Being eighteen, his body was mean and lean. He could have been on the cover of any American magazine. He had his dad's smile and eyes. More than thirty ladies of different ages waited for his run each day. Alex was as dark as Jere was light. At just under six feet, Alex, too, had the best body he would ever have. The two young men never noticed all the glances and leers. They were busy just being teens, surfing some of the time, or just swimming. They liked playing soccer and volleyball.

Verna, the manager of the Grand Palace, was one of those who admired their youth. Every morning, at 10:00, she and a couple of her friends would take coffee on the beach side of the hotel. They would talk about the birds and the weather and just watch Jere and Alex frolic some twenty feet away. To her left, she saw other ladies taking coffee, as well as to her right. For Jere and Alex, they were just enjoying the pleasures of Cancun. That would go for Verna and her friends also.

B en had called a meeting with all workers, including the nineteen captive girls. "Good morning, everyone. I'll be speaking in English, but we'll have translators talking with you in Spanish and Arabic. Today is a new day. My father the king, Ibrahim, is dead. His ship sank off the coast of Turkey. It didn't sink, but he needed to give a reason for the change. That makes me king of Balta. Next in line would be Rebecca. If anything should happen to me, then Rebecca would become ruler of Balta.

"Balta is an independent kingdom. My father ruled after his father. I'm not stupid. My father was both good and bad. As of today, some things will change, but most things will stay the same. I'm not 'Your Highness.' I'm Ben. The same is true with Rebecca. But I am the final word. The same rules that my father lived by still apply. If you are honest and work hard, then you will be rewarded. If you try to cheat me, then you will be rewarded. This is a private kingdom. No one can enter unless they are invited. That stays the same.

"Let me talk to you about the past couple of days. Adnan and my father were partners for decades, but Adnan wanted more. He stole billions from my father, and after my father left, I booted Adnan's people off the island. Adnan's people then attacked our island. They are now all dead. Adnan will join them soon. Now to everyone except the nineteen girls, you are excused."

It took twenty minutes for the room to clear out, except for the nineteen ladies. "Balta has been an island of refuge but also one of confinement. As of today, we end the confinement phase. You are free to come and go as you please. I say you are free to go. But if you go, you are on your own. If you are not on the island, I cannot protect you. In a couple of days, my attorneys will have papers for you to sign a nondisclosure agreement. I will pay you at least $1 million for your captivity. Some of you have been here for a while. You will get more. If you try to sue me, you will get nothing. I'm sorry for my father's stupid behavior, but I could do nothing until now. You can leave Balta today with nothing or tomorrow with one million. Once off the island, you become like everyone else. You cannot reenter without an invitation."

Adnan had some ears at the meeting that called him as soon as it was over. He was furious that the girls were being released. Adnan wanted the Mexican beauty Veronica. Now he would just take her again. He thought for a moment. The American would probably be with her. He would just capture them both when they left Balta.

He would send Tory, Tuttuu, and Yulie to pick up the girls. Rick and Hassan could still bring back two new girls, as planned. He would keep them all in Singapore. Adnan needed to keep Carlos with him to translate once they were on Cancun. Adnan had given in to his animalistic desires and was beginning a journey toward insanity. For Adnan, it would be a short trip.

S ara had money, while Veronica had none. So both girls stayed to get their Swiss bank account numbers. Then with only a small suitcase each, they walked onto the ferry for Bird Island. Bobby had been given a thousand dollars to call Tory when the girls left. "This will be my last phone call to you. My life is worth much more than a thousand dollars."

Tory knew life was changing on the island. He would worry about needing Bobby later. Right now, he needed to start an airplane and prepare for his trip to Singapore. "Tuttuu and Yulie, the girls are on the ferry. We don't need to go to them. They will come to us."

As the girls exited their cab, Tory was there to greet them. Tuttuu and Yulie grabbed their bags, while Tory flashed his Smith & Wesson. Tory ushered the girls out to the hangar where his plane was ready to fly to Singapore. "Ladies, get in, or else."

Sara didn't go quietly. She ran toward the hangar door. She heard "Stop, or I'll shoot!" Then she felt two blows in her back. Her world went black. She felt the ground hit her hard, and then she felt nothing. She thought, *So this is what dying is like.*

Tuttuu grabbed Veronica and slammed her into the back of the plane, and they took off. Sara's lifeless body lay in a pool of blood, not quite making it to freedom outside the hangar doors.

Ibrahim watched as the tug brought the *Verdi Mare* into the old port area of Istanbul. Unless you had connections, you didn't live very long there. Ibrahim had all the connections needed. He and his father had been trading here for a very long time. The docks smelled of fish and seaweed. Turkish was the tobacco of choice.

The *Verdi Mare* was tied up against old stones that might have seen some Roman ships at one time. The whole place was older than anyone could remember. When Maged stepped off the ship, he and Rick were both armed, and he left an armed guard on the ramp.

Maged was to meet up with Hassan, another captain for Adnan. Hassan led them to their meeting with Willow, an old gypsy working for Adnan. Standing next to her was Tuna, her guard. He stood 6'6". The Turks were growing them bigger these days. Tuna looked a bit like an *Aladdin* character without the rug. Very few words were spoken. Just a few papers signed. As captain of the ship, Maged had the authority to sign for goods. The money would flow electronically. With their business out of the way, Maged and Rick were taken to the baths. There they would soak, get a massage, and get some attention from some ladies.

In the morning, Rick was nowhere to be found. Maged made his way back to the docks, only to find his ship gone. That was why Hassan was in port. Hassan was now in charge of the *Verdi Mare*. Adnan had sent him to take over the ship. While Maged pondered his fate, a small boat with two Bird Island sailors on it pulled up to the big ancient stones. In Arabic, they hollered "Yalla, yalla" for him to hurry and get aboard. While he was thinking about it, they pointed to a ship not far off their port. Ibrahim was standing there with a big smile on his face.

Ibrahim waved for him to come on over. Maged wasn't sure he wanted to go. This might be his last boat ride. Ibrahim was not the forgiving sort, and he had just lost a boat. With nowhere else to go, Maged stepped into the skiff.

Maged saw a smiling Ibrahim. "Maged, what have you done with my ship?"

"Sir, I'm sorry, but I believe Rick and Hassan have taken your tanker."

"Don't worry. My friend, you have been betrayed. Actually, Rick works for me. Adnan works for himself, for a little while. The ship will stop in Africa and drop off the weapons for diamonds. It will then go to Mexico for propane at Matamoros and finally go to Cancun, but you know all of this as the ship's captain. We will be there to meet it. Come aboard."

It was as though Ibrahim knew what would happen. "How did you know they would replace me as captain?"

"Count your blessings, my friend. I thought they would just kill you and throw you off the ship. Maybe Rick had them just leave you. Anyway, you are alive."

The phone rang in the office, and Laura answered. "The Spirit Club."

"This is Sandra calling from Blackletters. I'm returning Mr. Allen's call."

Laura didn't know what she was talking about, so she handed the phone to Jack.

"This is Jack Allen."

"Yes, sir. I have Mr. Ponce for you."

"Okay."

Erik Ponce runs a semi-military civilian operations unit for hire. "Hello, Mr. Allen. I believe you were trying to reach me?"

"Yes. Can we meet?"

J ack's plane landed at Blackletters's private strip. A car drove out to the jet and picked up Jack. Only Victor made this trip with Jack. Things would be said and done that no one else needed to be in on. Next they were invited into the Ponce lair.

"Welcome, Mr. Fitzgerald—or should I call you Mr. Allen?"

"Call me Jack. This is my friend, Victor."

"Tell me why you are flying all the way to my little ranch from Cancun."

"The short story is that my daughter Sara and another girl were kidnapped from Cancun about a year ago. My private investigator got close and then got killed."

"Same people?"

"We are only guessing, but Johnny is dead. I think we are guessing correctly."

"How can I help you, Jack?"

"You can bring two girls back to Cancun."

"This will be very expensive. You will need to replace any equipment damaged during the ordeal."

"I can meet all of your terms."

"Jack, this is whether or not we bring the girls out. The costs will still be the same. Let's set aside one hundred million in an escrow account."

"Show Victor who to talk to, and I will tell you what I know."

Tonight Kate lay in bed thinking about all the complexities of motherhood. A few months ago, her home was busy with a lot of noise. Now it was too quiet. When Jere would catch a cold, Sara would fuss. "Does he have to breathe like that? It's driving me crazy."

"Honey, he has to breathe."

"Can he go breathe in his room?"

"Why can't she leave, Mom?"

Life was noisy but happy. The kids loved the pool. When the two were left alone, they had a good time together. Now the noise was gone, and so was the love. If Jack were to come back, this would be the perfect place to live.

Kate knew most of her friends were positional, because of her position at work and her money. They hid behind their masks. In the game of life, she was a princess. Isn't that what all little girls dream of becoming? In her garage sat a limo. Tony would drive her anywhere she wanted. She would always show up with him. He would hop out and open her door. Others would be watching with longing eyes. Kate appeared to have the perfect life. It was because she, too, kept her mask on.

Sunday,
OCTOBER 21, 2001

Hassan waited outside the harbor for his tugboat. Nothing would happen until Monday because most things were closed on Sunday. But that was okay. He had nothing better to do. The tanker was right on schedule.

Jack had decided to take both mothers on the raid if they chose to go. There would be rules they would have to agree to, or else they wouldn't be allowed to come along. Next he needed to talk with Frank about Kate missing work. He would talk to Kate face-to-face.

Ibrahim and his yacht had already docked at the Three Sisters Islands right next to Cancun. The sea and good company had already started improving his health. Cancer was going to end his life, but he could push that end a little further away.

J ack, Victor, and Laura flew to LaGuardia in New York. The next morning, Jack planned to visit Kate at the office. Victor simply went to his home in Queens. Jack and Laura stayed at the Courtyard by Marriott. Jack got a suite with two rooms.

"Jack, we don't need two rooms."

"Don't play right now. I'm already under enough stress."

"Yes, dear."

"On this trip, you can't call me dear."

"I want to go with you to see your company."

"That can happen, but not this trip. I've scheduled the spa treatment for you."

With the *Verdi Mare* anchored in the bay, most of the crew headed to the island of Cancun. Hassan found Adnan, and they discussed the best way to rid themselves of Ibrahim. Rick went to a pre-set meeting with Ibrahim. Then Rick headed off to the Spirit Club, looking for two new girls.

Rick spoke to Al, "You look familiar. Been working here long?"

Al tried not to jump or act excited—Rick had returned. "I've been here a few months. The place changed owners, and the new owner is Mr. Maddon from New York. Saw an offer online, and here I am."

"Seen any pickups?"

"Are you kidding? This is a tourist magnet. Come in tonight around nine." Al thought to himself, *Rick is looking for more girls to kidnap.* With Laura and Jack both gone, he would contact Captain Sanchez and Christi.

Victor and Jack headed to FGNY at the beginning of their day. Kate just caught a glimpse of Jack going past her office. Anne and her exchange glances. "This could be good." Kate hurried after him.

Jack and Victor walked right past Frank's secretary, Brenda, to greet Frank. "Hello, friend. When do you hand the company over to Steve?"

Frank shook their hands and then answered Jack's question. "He's taking some vacation time as we speak. When he returns, we'll announce it, and I walk out."

Kate's arrival closed that conversation. "Oh, hi, Jack, Victor. I didn't know you were coming by."

"Kate, that was intentional. Close the door, please. We need to talk to you." Jack continued, "This meeting is to invite you to take a trip with me, and others, of course. This has to do with our daughter. But I'll have some rules you must follow, or you can't come."

Wearing her mask, she acted shocked.

Jack continued, "One, no phone. Two, no questions. Three, Laura will be coming along, and so you can't act like a bitch. Four, no questions will be answered until we are underway. Five, you need casual clothes and a swimsuit."

Again, from behind her mask, she said, "I just can't leave right now. Things are in the works. I have meetings."

"Frank, can she walk out right now with me?"

"Of course, she can. Brenda, would you call Anne in here?"

"If you're going, I'll need your phone. We'll leave it with Frank." His hand was extended.

"I can't do this. I have to pack and other things."

"Everything you need can be found at the apartment. We'll go there next."

"Anne, Kate needs to leave us for a few days. Can you cover her department?"

"Sure. What's going on?"

No one answered Anne.

"Is Victor going with us?"

"What was number two? No questions. But no."

"But he can know and I can't?"

"Yes. Okay. Time's up. Let's go Victor. We'll get Laura on the way."

With Laura's name mentioned, Anne and Kate looked at each other with big eyes. Now Frank jumped in. "Phone."

"This is not fair." She was angry and happy. She grabbed her Jack's arm, and they were off to the apartment.

Jack's jet touched down at Bear Pen Airport, a tiny runway near the North Carolina coast. A taxi took the three travelers to Bowen Point Bar and Grill. That night, their lodging was at the Best Western.

Arriving bright and early in the morning, a van with a newly printed sign, Vikings Executive Micro Tours, picked up the threesome. A small ship had been purchased from a friend of Mr. Ponce and had been reconditioned during the week. Three Black Hawk helicopters were hidden below deck. The deck had a small swimming pool and other cruise amenities. The staff actually worked for the cruise line that sold Erik the ship. The SWAT team all wore civilian clothing, disguised as tourists on a cruise. A dozen ladies had accepted a free cruise to Jakarta.

The man in charge introduced himself as General Alec. In fact, he was a retired Navy SEAL, and the rest didn't matter. The first stop was a briefing room. Jack was talking to his two lady companions. "Ladies, we are on a mission to try and set our two daughters free." He told them about all the intel that had been gathered, up to the point of the cost of the expedition and who was going to do the rescuing. "The truth is, we don't know if they were ever there or if they are still there."

Kate was skeptical. "Where is 'there'?"

"Fair question. We are going to a small island in the Molucca Sea run by one family for the last one hundred years, Balta. It's located near Indonesia, but is not part of Indonesia. A short distance away is an island called Bird. Our investigator was on Bird and was getting too close to them, so they killed him. The police chief said as much, as he closed the investigation. The people on Balta are pirates. They don't follow the same rules we follow. The king of the island is named Ibrahim.

"We are using this ship as a cover so we can get in close. We will go in and not leave without word on the girls. You don't need to know the details, but we are getting to watch it live on these three screens. Kate and I spared no expense to find our girls."

"I haven't spent any money."

"Not yet, but you will. I'm sure you'll want to share the expenses."

Laura was in tears, while Kate was in disbelief. "So much effort on so little evidence." In front of Laura, Kate was still wearing her mask. Underneath, she was afraid to let herself have any hope.

Jack replied to Kate, "Exactly."

Rick himself placed the explosives on Ibrahim's yacht. The crew was staying at a hotel on the island of the Three Sisters. Dr. Hung, Maged, and Ibrahim all appeared to board his yacht, as Adnan pushed the remote button and blew it up. Actually, the three gentlemen had boarded a small skiff and were being taken to safety. Now dead, Ibrahim could move freely.

Adnan smiled widely. All his fears and frustrations with the old pirate Ibrahim were now taken care of. Many thoughts raced through his head. *Should I try to take over Balta? Should I try and steal more tankers? Should I . . .* But first he had to capture his new girls and get them away from Cancun.

Rick was at the Spirit Club and was implementing his plan. At the Spirit Club, Rick had selected two sisters from Texas, Cynthia and Alicia Hopkins. As they paid their bill, he added a small package of heroin to one purse. Next he followed them to their hotel. Maria Longoria was working with him to bring in the drug users.

Al phoned Christi, and the double trap was underway. Christi stayed way behind Rick and Officer Longoria.

Around midnight, the sisters entered the Hyatt and went straight to their room. Officer Longoria went straight to the front desk and, showing her ID, asked for the room number of the notorious Hopkins sisters. The clerk was glad to help a police officer out. Maria quickly made it to room 617. "Police! Open the door!"

Stunned, Alicia opened the door. Maria entered like a gust of wind, her nine mil out and pointed at Alicia. "On the floor!"

Still in shock, Cynthia and Alicia hit the floor. Maria cuffed them with their hands behind their backs. Next she found the heroin bag. "Okay, ladies. You've got some explaining to do to the judge. Grab your purses, and let's go."

Still stunned, the sisters did as they were told. Maria had phoned Rick and gave the room number. Rick had parked the *policia* van off a side hallway, so the clerk never saw them leave. Rick fastened them in the van and placed hoods over their heads. That's when the girls knew they were being kidnapped.

Cynthia started screaming, and Rick gave her a left cross.

"What did you do to my sister?"

"I gave her a left cross. Would you like one?"

"You can't get away with this!"

Rick gave her a left cross as well. Then he gave a shot to knock out both girls for about twelve hours. Next he switched the magnetic signs. The policia van became a tourist taxi.

Christi caught everything on video. She then followed the van to the port. There she also recorded the girls being placed in a container that was then lifted onboard the *Verdi Mare*.

Noe couldn't believe his good fortune. Carlos had come calling with $25,000 in cash. "Noe, don't let anything stop us from leaving port tonight."

"Nothing will stop you, I promise."

N oe had given the tug driver $5,000 to turn off his radio. Captain Sanchez was screaming into the microphone, but the tug kept moving with the *Verdi Mare*. Captain Sanchez was moving to plan B. As he left the port authority's office, he fell back against the wall and then to the ground. The sharpshooter's bullet had put the captain down. The *Verdi Mare* was forgotten, and lifesaving procedures began for the captain.

Rick was not on the ship. He had been watching from a safe distance, but he saw the captain fall. Next an ambulance appeared with its lights flashing. Then the lights were turned off. The captain was dead.

Ship Captain Hassan sailed on. The sisters were leaving the Americas and were heading for their new home, Singapore. Cynthia and Alicia were still sleeping and would wake up as slaves of a madman. Carlos had hired Maria Longoria to take care of the girls and eventually be in charge of Adnan's harem. The girls were to be left in Maria's care.

Noe stopped by the policia station to take over as the new chief. There was a lot of action going on Halloween morning. "Hey, guys, what's going on?"

Pedro Salas was wearing the captain's rank. "Hello, Noe, what are you doing here?"

"Why are you wearing captain's rank?"

"Orders from Captain Sanchez."

"Hey, if something has happened to Sanchez, then I'm next in authority. Take that rank off."

"By orders from Captain Sanchez, if anything should happen to him tonight, I'm to be promoted, and you are to be arrested."

Suddenly, Noe began acting like a captured wild lion. But before he could escape, he was cuffed, and his weapon was removed. "You won't get away with this, Salas. I have friends."

"No, you have no friends. We tried to bring in Maria, but she's gone. We are not letting you use the phone, and no one knows you've been arrested. You will stay in confinement until you go before a judge and after that as well. All of this will be done in secret. Oscar, take this piece of trash away."

"Wait. You have to tell me why I'm being arrested."

"There are too many to list, but how about murdering Captain Sanchez? Or how about taking that bribe from Carlos Borego. What did our informant say, $25,000?"

Carlos and Adnan were at the airport now, waiting for a flight back to Singapore. Captain Salas knew their names but had no idea what they looked like. Their false identities had been created years earlier for this very reason.

Officially, Ibrahim was dead and Jake Goldman was alive, so it was easy for Jake to move around. Dr. Hung was also a pirate with another identity, Ho Kim of Taiwan. Only Maged had to create a new identity. Ibrahim, or Jake Goldman, knew some people who could fix Maged up. He became Kareem Sultan of Iraq. Now the three were ready to retire. Jake was not happy Adnan had slipped out of the trap. Jake would have to trust Ben to take care of his old partner. Meanwhile, Jake was looking for a new yacht to buy.

Rick had rejoined Jake on the Three Sisters Islands. Rick went back to his real name, Alex Brand. Quietly, Jake bought another nice boat, and the four men headed off into retirement.

T wo weeks of sailing brought the Vikings cruise ship into the sea of Molucca. This was the most boring time Kate had spent. Her phone had been taken from her. She couldn't contact Anne to see how things were going. Kate realized she couldn't live in Cancun. Either Jack would come back to his real life in New York City or they would part company. She was ready for some action, and it would soon come.

General Alec was not a general because he was a civilian. But he could call himself whatever he wanted because he was in charge. Preparations had been made, and rehearsals had been run. Tomorrow the raid would happen. The twelve men by the pool were gone. Now only ladies surrounded the pool.

The twelve ladies, winners of the free trip to Jakarta, were ready for Jakarta. Two weeks at sea was kind of boring. The men had all been interesting but not very much into relationships. There had been some sex but absolutely no relational commitments.

Jack had kept an eye on his two ladies. Kate needed her phone and something to do. Laura calmly read her books and relaxed. Jack knew Kate would not be staying away from the Big Apple.

On the *Verdi Mare*, life was normal for everyone except the two sisters. They were imprisoned in some very nice quarters, but it was still a jail. Maria could come and go as she chose, but the sisters only had one hour a day up on the deck and under guard.

Veronica was also under guard twenty-four hours a day. She had lost Sara because Sara ran. Now Sara was dead. Veronica wondered if that was not preferable to being a prisoner for life. With Sara's life snuffed out, there went Veronica's slim hope of being rescued. Adnan had been back a week, and he had used her every night.

J ack woke up the ladies very early in the morning. He told them the action would begin in ten minutes. He then went to the briefing room and sat down, waiting for the action to begin. Laura joined him first, and then Kate. In the briefing room, they could hear the commands but had no input. The operational command post was in a different room upstairs.

General Alec began the operation by launching all three helicopters. A GPS could also be used for imagery. Alec had chosen one building off by itself. It was 0500 hours, so it was probably not in use. The air-to-ground smart bomb woke up the isle.

Immediately, Ali Al Mutari launched his helicopters. This is what Alec had been waiting for. Now he knew the frequency they were on and could talk to them.

"If you want to keep those choppers, I recommend you shut them down. We have them targeted and will blow them up. Over."

"Who am I talking with?"

"It doesn't matter who I am. I could have blown up half your island. I chose a building not in use to get your attention. I'm coming in as we speak. Stand down now, or I will blow up everything."

Ben spoke. "Come in." He wanted to say a lot more but didn't. He quickly ran to where the choppers were coming in. Ali and Yosef were not happy with his decision, but they deferred.

Only one chopper had landed; three people came forward.

Again Ben spoke. "What gives you the right to attack us?"

"We are not here to negotiate or explain anything. Two other choppers are in the air still, and you are targeted. Very briefly, we've come for Sara and Veronica. Either you give them up or we start blowing things up."

"Sara and Veronica were here, but they left."

"I'm sorry, but that's the wrong answer. I guess we need to start blowing things up."

"Wait. I said they left. A rogue member, Adnan, tried to kidnap both girls over on Bird Isle. He got Veronica, but Sara panicked and tried to run. She should have died, but she didn't. She's alive and in our clinic here. If you have a medical person with you, then you can have her. If you don't, then I recommend leaving her here."

"You need to prepare her for travel right now. I have a medical technician. Tell me where your Adnan took Veronica."

Back in the briefing room, Kate had begun crying. Sara was alive and coming onboard the ship. She looked at Laura and knew her pain. Veronica was still out there. The two hugged. Kate took off her mask for a little while.

"Fly me back to your command center, and we can talk. Ali and Yosef, please come with me."

The extraction went smoothly. Within minutes, all three choppers landed back on deck. Jack and the two ladies were told to stay put. Finally, after some twenty minutes, a pale Sara was wheeled in on a stretcher. First, Kate went to Jack and said, "Thank you for not giving up. We have our daughter back." Then came her hug.

To Sara, she said, "Thank God you are alive. Your dad never gave up hope." Then came a modified hug because of Sara's condition.

Father and daughter just looked at each other. "Hello, Sara."

"Hello, Daddy."

There were smiles and tears all throughout the room.

Laura was happy for the Fitzgerald family, but her story wasn't finished yet. Veronica was in Singapore. There was no plan for her yet.

Sara's wounds would take months to heal, but they would heal. Adnan left her for dead, and she nearly did die.

Ben was taken to see Alec. "Besides my building you destroyed, we have a problem. Adnan has stolen billions from our family over the years. Recently, he reregistered five tankers under his rogue company. Their headquarters is located in Singapore. You can't go in there blowing things up. On the other hand, I think I can take him out. That means getting Veronica out as well. Are you interested in staying in Singapore for, say, a week?"

"I don't have orders past our action today. But my men deserve some time off. The answer is yes."

Alec needed to get permission to dock. His ship had not been expected. Ben knew the port authority personnel and got them to let the *Viking Executive Micro Cruise* dock for a small fee of $15,000. Now the winners and the crew members could really party and take in the sights. Jack and Kate had in front of them their point of interest. Laura was not in the mood to be a tourist.

Alec notified Jack that the *Verdi Mare* would be in port on Friday. There were no plans to do anything to it, just FYI.

Ali and Yosef were in charge of the raid on the Eastern Green Sea Shipping Corporation. Their rented CH-47 Chinook, a twin rotor chopper, took them and fifteen of the island's special guards to the top of Century Towers, a ninety-five-story building. Adnan occupied the whole ninety-second floor. No one could enter without the proper identification card, unless you carried some plastic explosives. These explosives had a big pop with only a small amount of smoke.

The Chinook landed on the roof, and the tailgate came down. The team ran down three flights of stairs to the ninety-second floor. Three guards were dead before they knew what hit them. Seventeen people entered the headquarters of EGSSC. About forty workers looked up and saw the combat team enter, and they knew their lives were about to change.

The team quickly spread out through the floor, bringing the three most important people out to meet with Ali and Yosef. Adnan might have been the most surprised person on the floor. He had located his business back in the civilized world thinking no pirate could touch him here.

Carlos Borega was the first to speak. "This is an outrage!" He didn't get to finish his speech. Ali shot him.

Next Ali addressed Adnan, pointing his gun at his face, "Our first demand is that I need all three girls here within ten minutes."

In one last bluster, Adnan said, "That's impossible. That's not going to happen. You are crazy if you think—" That's all he got out before Ali shot him in the face, and he dropped like a rock.

"Okay, Estaben. Are you willing to work with me? I might be crazy, but if you do what I say, you will live."

"I think I can work with you."

"Good. Send one man with Yosef to bring the girls back here."

"Abel, show these pirates where the girls are."

Yosef and five guards went with Abel to the harem chamber and returned with the three ladies.

"Yosef told you, I'm sure, but we are indeed freeing you. Veronica, Sara is alive, and we are working with her father to free you. Alicia and Cynthia, I'm sure that there is room on the boat for you as well."

Looking at the girls, Yosef pointed to one of the guards and said, "Follow him to the chopper." To the office workers, he said, "Green Sea just died. You need to clear out of this building and go find a job. I wouldn't talk with the police. They might wonder why you were working for pirates. Estaben, we need you and three of your best workers to come with us as well. If we are happy with your work, you will live."

Estaben pointed to three of his people, and the four followed the team to the roof.

Mike was the last of the Balta guards to clear the room. Once on the Chinook, they all relaxed. Helmets and body armor all came off. Weapons were passed down to the crate for storage.

Now with a headset on, Yosef asked the copilot to connect him with Alec. "Alec, we were successful and would like to drop off three ladies on our way back to Balta. In exchange, how about donating one million to rebuild our gym?"

"Done."

Jack knew but didn't say anything about the rescue, in case it didn't happen. Lounging at the pool with Laura, Jack saw the Chinook land. Laura looked at Jack as if to say, *What is this?* "Stay put. Let's see."

The two sisters were the first off, and then Veronica. Laura was up and running. She almost tumbled. There were hugs and kisses and jumping around. The chopper lifted off without anyone else getting off.

Speaking to her mother in Spanish, Veronica asked, "Where is Mr. Fitzgerald?"

Laura just pointed toward Jack. Veronica ran to him and held on, crying even more. She managed to whisper, "Thank you."

With that, Jack had his reward.

Laura looked at him and knew she was blessed.

The *Viking Executive Micro Cruise* ship jolted as it began to leave port. The Chinook took off, heading back to Balta. The guards would be dropped off and the CH-47 returned.

Her face had been buried in Jack's chest. Veronica looked up then and said, "They said Sara is on board."

Jack just nodded.

"Can we go see her?"

"The short answer is yes, but remember, she's torn up inside."

"I know. I thought she was dead."

Together, the three of them went to see Sara.

"Sara, look who I found." She was referring to Jack.

"See, I told you he would look."

Laura forgot about the rules and held on to her Jack.

Speaking to Sara, Jack said, "By the way, Sara, Al told me to tell you hello."

www.ingramcontent.com/pod-product-compliance
Lightning Source LLC
Chambersburg PA
CBHW050452110726
47899CB00003B/906